It must have been McNutt

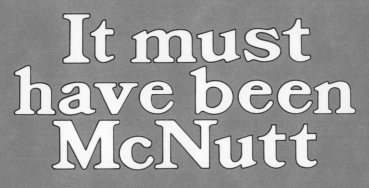

Illustrated by Kathy Kushe and David Hastings

Bryan Jeffery Leech
and
Glenn Edward Sadler

G/L
REGAL
BOOKS

A Division of G/L Publications
Glendale, California, U.S.A.

Published by
Regal Books Division, G/L Publications
Glendale, California 91209, U.S.A.

Library of Congress Catalog Card No. 73-93579
ISBN 0-8307-0288-1

April 2nd 1976

To Dick & Betsy,

From "McNutt"
and one of his kin —

Bryan Telbey [signature]

Dedication

To all Brients, Barrs and Buteyns,
all Sadlers, Bearingers and Thomases,
and all other friends of wee folk.
B.L. *and* G.S.

CHAPTER 1

A Bad Day for the Broonies

"It's a bad day for the Broonies," sighed Grady, the cook, for the third time that morning. Her breakfast rolls had stuck again to the pan, putting her in a bad mood.

"But who *are* the Broonies?" repeated Addie Bradbourne, who was helping to lay the table in the dining room and had come into the kitchen to fetch her father's favorite marmalade.

"I really don't know," replied Grady, "the questions you *do ask*, child. It's just an expression me mother used and her mother before her and it helps me not to say things I might be regrettin'."

"But do you think there *really are* such things, Grady?" asked the youngster quite seriously.

"Why of course there are—" the cook hesitated, "me cousin Milty McGoon claimed that he once saw one—*where* and *how*, well that I can't say. But hurry up now, dearie, or your father will be most unhappy with both of us," she concluded, patting the child's head with her floury hand.

Breakfast proceeded nearly on schedule. The rector of All Hallows Church ate heartily, complimenting Grady on her rolls when they finally appeared after his second cup of coffee. This made her feel better. After he had read the *Boston Globe* and his wife, Melissa, had noted the social events for the week in the *Perry-Dutton Gazette*, the family dispersed. Mrs. Bradbourne went to give daily instructions to Miss Nemma Smidgin, the family governess who was in charge of the welfare of Addie, her sister and her two brothers. The rector retired to his study, closing the door firmly behind him.

Outside the study door Addie paused. In spite of her father's request that he not be disturbed, she tapped lightly. At first there was no reply. But then, as she continued,

4

her father called out, rather shortly, "Yes, who is it? What do you want? Come in, come in!"

When no one entered, he got up and went to the door, expecting the new housemaid who had no doubt come to dust up (and he hated being dusted). Removing his wire spectacles, his face brightening when he saw his youngest daughter, he waved her into the room and seated her in an enormous leather chair across from his desk. And he offered her a barley sugar from a small amber jar that he kept hidden in one of the lower drawers.

It was nearing the time of Addie's tenth birthday, and for two weeks she had been hinting at a certain China doll which she had seen on a shopping expedition in the Curio Shop near Beacon Hill. Patiently, her father waited.

"Well, my dear, what is it you want?" he asked, peering over his glasses with an amused glint in his eyes.

"Nothing really, Papa. But, well, yes—there *is* something I want to know. Perhaps you can help."

From Addie's somber expression her father sensed that she was not thinking about birthdays. "Go ahead, child, tell me," he encouraged her.

"You see," she began cautiously, "Grady keeps talking about Broonies all the time, and I've asked her about them—and—and—I want to know where they live. And, Papa, why is it a 'bad day for the Broonies' and where is Seton Woods and why did they flee from Scotland to Ireland and. . . ."

Addie paused, looking up at her father as she did every Sunday in church; from his sermons she had gained the impression that he must know everything.

Mr. Bradbourne contemplated, paused and twisted his lapels and looked at her rather vaguely. His hobby, when he found time for it, was collecting books on British history.

But about Broonies, he had only the slightest notion of who or what they were.

"You mean Brownies, *Scots Brownies,* don't you, dearie?" he asked.

"No! Papa, Grady calls them Broonies," Addie insisted.

"Yes, I suppose that Broonies *is* what Grady would call them . . . those curious wee folk, related to Leprechauns, so I am told. There are, you know, many strange stories about them. But I, myself, am not sure what to think. We must be careful not to believe all the things we hear, Addie."

But seeing his daughter's dissatisfaction with his explanation, he continued: "Well, if it will make you happy, I'll write to my good friend Mr. Joseph Sean-Ticky in Ireland and ask him what he knows about Broonies. He's very good at finding out all there is to know about all sorts of things."

"Thank you, Papa," said Addie, slipping off the chair and preparing to leave. "Perhaps he can even send a Broonie to live with us," added the child.

And with that she opened the door to the study and soon was out in the garden, her mind on other things.

CHAPTER 2

Mr. Sean-Ticky's Alarming Discovery

Sean-Ticky, Sean-Ticky & Sons (Booksellers) by appointment to Her Majesty Queen Victoria had become a permanent fixture of the High Street, Londonderry, Northern Ireland. The bookshop's future was, however, somewhat uncertain since Mr. Sean-Ticky (Mr. Joseph as he was affectionately called) was still—at age 45—a bachelor.

Mr. Joseph was always punctual. The door opened at precisely 9:00 A.M. and was closed promptly at 6:00 P.M. sharp. Between these hours business was conducted swiftly but quietly. It was the pride of Mr. Sean-Ticky that customers could browse in his shop in an atmosphere as undisturbed as the shuffled calm of the Londonderry Free Public Library. Also he boasted that he could find any volume, upon special request, within a month—even books of the rarest kind. And such was his reputation that British and American requests were frequently sent to him for the seemingly unobtainable.

The bane of Mr. Joseph's life was Harry O'Neill, the postman. He could never predict when Harry would arrive, and when he did finally burst into the hushed quiet of the shop, he would be lustily whistling "The Kerry Dance" or some other common air.

"This shop reminds me of a sittin'-room during a wake," complained Harry when reproached by Mr. Joseph for making another noisy entrance. Then to Mr. Joseph's annoyance, he refused to hand over the post.

"Now *that's* what I call an interestin' letter!" he exclaimed, holding a large envelope well out of the reach of Mr. Joseph who stood only five-feet-two to Harry's six-feet-one.

"Aye, 'tis at that," responded Mr. Joseph slyly, "but since ye cannot read, I fail to understand yer fascination wi' it . . . here, Harry," ventured the bookseller, "let me give ye a fresh pipeful of Heather & Thistle." And Mr. Joseph disappeared into the interior of the shop. Soon he returned with Harry's favorite brand of tobacco.

Mr. Joseph snatched the letter from the postman as soon as Harry had sat down to stuff his pipe. "Someday I *will* report ye, Harry O'Neill, for yer cheeky ways," muttered Mr. Sean-Ticky as he tore open the American stamped letter and gestured Harry toward the door before he could fill the shop with tobacco smoke.

Except for the tinkle of the front door, the postman left without another sound.

The letter, as Mr. Joseph expected, was from The Reverend Cornelius Bradbourne of Perry-Dutton, Massachusetts, one of his best customers, whose ancestors came from Ireland. Excitedly, Mr. Joseph ran his eyes over the long list of titles. "There must be at least ten—maybe fifteen items," counted the bookseller eagerly, "and I can put my finger on all of them."

But then his expression changed. "What is this!" he queried, "I've never heard of. . . ." Mr. Joseph stopped short, calling Davis Ryan, his assistant. "Ryan, come here! Have ye ever heard of *The Laws, Customs and Deeds of the Little People, Being a Truthful Account of Their Origin and Habits?*"

"No, indeed, I can't rightly say that I have," replied the other.

"He's always ordering odd things. This one must be for Grady. She was always talking about the 'wee ones'—even when she was mother's maid and Milty McGoon was the gardener," Mr. Joseph muttered to himself.

Mr. Sean-Ticky and his assistant spent the remainder of the day rummaging through back rooms and checking neglected storage cupboards. Frequently Mr. Joseph dashed back into his office to consult his prize collection of refer-

11

ence materials on Irish lore. In one source, he discovered—quite to his surprise—an account by a Sir Franklyn Shea, distinguishing between two separate races of "wee folk": the Leprechauns and the Brownies.

At the bottom of the yellowed page in very fine print, he read:

> "There is reportedly also a small sept clan of Brownies whose habits and origin are uncertain. They have been called by some the Broonies of Seton Woods."

"How very odd that I've never heard of the Seton Woods Broonies," whispered Mr. Joseph to himself.

But relieved to find an excuse for his ignorance, he read on:

> "Now as everyone knows, Leprechauns and Broonies are quite separate beings. Unlike Leprechauns, who have always been rather plentiful, Broonies (as they are called by men folk) appear small in number and in size. In stature they rarely reach beyond two feet. Instead of being known for impish pranks, or for searching for crocks of gold, Broonies are of an entirely different disposition and quite neglect the acquisition of wealth. They are said now to be extremely generous and some have been decorated by the Crown for conspicuous acts of gallantry in times of war and for philanthropic gestures during times of peace."

The chronicle went on to discuss the physical characteristics of the Seton Woods Broonies: "In appearance they are elflike, of diminutive size but with adult features of a peculiarly tannish color which fades to a pale green when they are confronted with disbelief or when they remember the Koppelbacks. They are inclined to be plump, rather bowlegged and poorly coordinated, tumbling over each other while romping through the fields and woods. But when this happens, as it often does, they laugh about it, such is their irrepressible sense of humor.

"Broonies are extremely musical. Their night songs sound like high-pitched bagpipes, strongly dissonant and in the minor key. Often they sing of Umbrie, their Scottish homeland, from which they were cruelly expelled by the Koppelbacks of Grimmelgower, one-legged giants who took their wives and children away into captivity.

"Where Umbrie is now, the Broonies cannot recall, yet they are constantly singing of it. During the day they are silent, however, and hardly speak, so devoted are they to their work of gaining 'moments of belief,' an ancient custom which is essential to their livelihood. Otherwise, these Broonies beam broadly and chuckle over private jokes.

"It's a bad day for the Broonies," exclaimed Mr. Sean-Ticky, closing the heavy volume and replacing it carefully. "Ryan!" he called, "at least I know something of who they are—these Broonies of Seton Woods—but this is the first time I've ever heard of such a volume. I can't think where to find it . . . unless Lady Angela or one of the other members of The Society should possess a copy. It's a calamity, it is, if I have to disappoint Mr. Bradbourne."

Hovering over a large stack of water-stained journals, Davis Ryan, perched on the top of a ladder, turned peevishly toward his employer, as the ladder swayed.

"Aye, so it is, so it is," he replied, coughing in a whirl of dust with a weariness that betrayed little sympathy with his employer's interest in little people.

The rest of the day was spent tidying up.

CHAPTER 3

The Meeting at Ballybligh

The next meeting of "The Society for the Advancement of Little People, Their Friends and Kin" took place on the following Thursday evening. The distinguished group, of which Mr. Joseph was a charter member and the present presiding officer, met once a month, always on the first full moon, for a midnight supper at Ballybligh. This was the home of Lady Angela Foggerty, an eccentric novelist who had now written twenty-three romances, none of which had yet been published. She lived in a spacious four-storied house, overlooking the River Sorral, providing a fine view of Seton Woods. There she claimed to have more than an "occasional acquaintance" with the wee folk—elves, gnomes, gambols and others of their kind.

In keeping with her book-scattered house, Lady Angela's appearance was grand but bedraggled. Her gown was peppered with brooches, as if they were holding it together, which they probably were, and her hair was stacked with a mass of pins and clips. Invariably, she was seen with at least one cat draped over her shoulder like a living boa, and frequently she would break off her conversation with a guest to talk to it—thus confusing both the cat and the guest. A visitor might be alarmed to think that he was being congratulated for being a good rat-catcher or that he was being asked if he had enjoyed his nap, when actually Her Ladyship was talking to a Siamese or tabby around her neck and not to the guest at all.

"And what did you say, my dear?" asked Mrs. Brudge, the only other lady present.

"I said that you ask far too many questions, Mrs. Brudge," replied Lady Angela. "Can't you listen to the proceedings without constantly inserting your own opinion?"

"I'll try, my dear Angela, I really wish I could. I simply *must try,*" consented Mrs. Brudge, pointing her chin even higher into the air and trying not to be intimidated by her hostess.

The meeting of The Society was always preceded by a hearty supper of Donegal stew (Lady Angela's own recipe) and shamrock tarts with plenty of Irish coffee or tea afterwards. The eleven members ate in the long, narrow dining room, facing the river. After the last sip of tea had been taken, and as the men were puffing contentedly on briar pipes while the ladies were clicking their knitting needles, Mr. Sean-Ticky presented the issue at hand.

Having dispensed with old business, he continued: "Ladies and gentlemen, if I may have yer attention now. We have before us a most important request from The Reverend Cornelius Bradbourne of Perry-Dutton, Massachusetts. His letter has, in fact, disrupted me whole working day and. . . ."

"Yes! yes!" interjected Lady Angela, "we are fully aware of the difficulties under which you work—but *that* is not the question, is it? Now my dear Mr. Joseph, please continue."

"That's what I say," added Mrs. Brudge. "It seems to me that what should be done. . . ." But here Mrs. Brudge halted, having forgotten in the midst of her speculation what she was saying.

Ignoring both ladies, Mr. Joseph read Mr. Bradbourne's letter. "We have been challenged," he concluded. "The reputation and future of our Society is at stake if we can't find this wee book. Does anyone know if such a book actually exists?"

A long pause followed as each member stared at the others. The men stopped smoking while both ladies knitted when they should have purled.

Finally the silence was broken by a gruff voice. Struggling

gawkily to his feet and speaking in a deliberate tone, Captain Blewsby, the past president of The Society and its senior member, began. "I, for one, I mean speaking for myself, I can see no reason why *I* should not be able to discover the missing volume in my library. It is, as you all know, endless in its resources and I have just recently added a very fine collection of. . . ."

"But my dear William," chimed the ladies at once, "we *all* have fine libraries and collections which are equally famous. The point is: does this particular book exist? I can . . . er . . . we can never recall having even heard of it. A book on the Seton Woods Broonies—it would indeed be curious!"

On a sudden impulse Lady Angela jumped to her feet. A large Angora asleep beside her leapt into the air, putting Mrs. Brudge into a fright. Then marching out of the large living room, Her Ladyship commanded the others to follow her.

CHAPTER 4

Into the
Seton Woods

Handing a lantern to each of the men as they left the lengthy porch of Ballybligh, and indicating to her manservant to lead the way, Lady Angela ushered her excited guests along a gravel path and struck out for the garden, down into a narrow grassy meadow and toward a large copse of trees which guarded the woods beyond.

Approaching a dense grove of oaks of such magnitude that the full moon and sparkling stars were blotted out, the company moved deeper into the woods, thankful for the flickering light of the lanterns. As they came finally to a large clearing surrounded by young pines, Lady Angela cautioned them to stop.

"Wait here," she whispered.

In obedience they halted.

Above her, perched on a long pine branch partially blocking their view, sat a large horned owl, staring down at the strange intruders. Recognizing Lady Angela, it blinked three times—as if in greeting—and flew silently to a lower branch, where it waited. For several minutes they consorted—the owl hooting softly as Lady Angela nodded back in agreement.

Suddenly the owl began flapping its wings and a look of alarm crossed Lady Angela's face. Motioning the others to remain behind, she sped through the trees, following the snowy white bird as it flew deeper and deeper into the forest. Soon only the bobbing of Lady Angela's lantern could be seen, disappearing into the distant darkness of the pines.

Faintly, she perceived the rising drone of the warm night wind and the merest suggestion of chanting. Higher and higher it soared. She listened intently and, as she did so, an eerie humming tone sounded in her ears, bringing tears to eyes that seldom cried.

The owl beckoned her further on into the darkness. She

followed obediently. At last she came to a clearing in the forest. In its center stood a large circle of twelve massive oaks. Beneath her feet she felt the cushioned softness of the yellow-green moss, filling the glade in front of her. Stealthily she moved toward the nearest oak in order to examine it more closely. Bending down, Lady Angela noticed that a large hole, some three feet high, had been cut into the solid wood and that the inside of the gnarled tree had been hollowed out, as if to make room for some tiny creature.

Each of the trees in the circle had, in turn, been converted into miniature apartments. There were several knotholes in the upper part of the trunk, carved out for windows. "How very clever they are," thought Lady Angela, "I only wish I were taller so that I could peep inside them." On the nearest branches rows of small hammocks swung gaily in the night breezes and several tiny garments were hanging out to dry.

The owl, who had momentarily disappeared, now flew down and perched himself on the rim of one of the tree openings, beckoning her to approach. Then he flew off again toward another tree at the far side of the circle. As Lady Angela followed him, she could see that he was directing her to a window-knot high up in the trunk of a certain oak where a light was burning in one of the small casements.

Gingerly, but with remarkable strength for her age, she clambered up a tiny ladder made of used rope, which had been hung on the side of the giant oak. At last she managed to reach the security of a large branch from which she could peer into the opening. Peeping cautiously through it, she saw, several feet below her, a tiny dwarfish man sitting on a stool with his back to her. He was busily working.

The room was obviously his workshop. Benches and other

assorted pieces of furniture lay scattered about, in the process of being mended. Industriously he worked, gluing together a chair which was almost twice his size, while chanting a tune. Lady Angela could just barely hear the words:

"Awake, awake brave singing kin;
Awake, awake your song begin:
Tell us, tell us, Broonie friend
How best our foolish ways to mend. . . ."

"What a curiosity he is," exclaimed Lady Angela to herself, "so bowlegged, and his face—that tomato-colored nose and tannish skin—and look at those curly reddish sideburns. They form a single curl instead of a beard! I'll wager even the other Little People must laugh at him!"

As Lady Angela was debating with herself over how to attract his attention and how, in fact, one should properly address such an extraordinary personage, the branch to which she was clinging began to shake violently.

"Help, oh, someone help me, help! I'm falling," she cried.

Down Lady Angela fell, rolling onto the mossy floor of the clearing, narrowly missing two large roots of the giant oak. For a few moments she lay stunned at the base of the trunk. When she opened her eyes, the same funny little man stood over her.

"Nice of ye to drop in," he said, with a slight grin. "I trust there are no bones broken—we planted the moss there just in case of such a mishap."

Rubbing herself indignantly and blushing with embarrassment, Lady Angela ordered him to help her up. "You may please assist me," she demanded. "I didn't come into the forest at this hour of the night to trade jests with you—and just who *are* you, may I ask?"

She did not allow time for him to reply. "Now let's get to the point: I'm Lady Angela Foggerty of Ballybligh, and I've come here with the hope of meeting one of the Broonies of Seton Woods—I don't suppose you're one of them?"

"*I?* Why *I* am Shamus McNutt," he replied with a jaunty toss of his head. "And Yer Ladyship has indeed come to the right place, for I am the only Broonie about in the woods tonight. All me brothers is out on expeditions of a sort throughout the countryside. For while ye big folk sleep, Me Lady, we are out doing what ye leave undone. You'll forgive me for not receiving ye with the proper attention, but it isn't usual for us to be spied on in our own wee homes by the likes of ye."

Assuming an embarrassed expression, Lady Angela managed for once to speak with gentleness. "I apologize, Mr. McNutt, my intention was not to sneak up on you—I meant no harm. But fearing how very sensitive you Broonies might be and your dislike of being seen, I felt it only proper—I mean, I tried to approach you carefully. I thought your little town was quite deserted, before I looked into your tree window."

"Thank ye, Ma'am," said McNutt, bowing cheerfully. "Ye need not explain more, now that I understand yer intentions. I'm indeed glad to welcome ye to me wee house, which few find. I would like to take Yer Ladyship inside, which would be fittin', but ye simply would nay fit," he chuckled and bowed again politely.

Taking her hand gently, the little man led her to an opening in the trees, where the moonlight revealed a large stump projecting up from the mossy floor. There he motioned for her to rest. Swiftly he climbed the rope-ladder and disappeared into his workshop, returning soon with two small tankards full of mulled greenberry wine.

25

Lady Angela took a sip, savored it, and then began her story. "You see, my dear Mr. McNutt," she began, "our Society, of which you have no doubt heard, has received a most urgent request from a Reverend Cornelius Brad-bourne of Perry-Dutton, Massachusetts, an American gentleman and one of Mr. Sean-Ticky's best customers—a great lover of books. It seems that his youngest daughter—I believe her name is Adeline. . . ."

"Yes, Me Lady," interrupted Shamus, "we know the family well and, in fact, at this very minute one of our best scouts has taken up residence in their garden, a loyal and trusted comrade. . . ."

"Well, as I was saying, Mr. McNutt," continued Lady Angela, "we have been asked to locate a certain book, one which gives—so we are told—an account of your kinfolk, their origin and customs. I don't have to tell you, I am sure, how very important it is to us as a Society that we find it."

She paused expectantly.

"Aye, Me Lady, I see that ye are indeed in—I think ye say, 'a pickle,' and methinks you've come to the right place. But then one always comes to that which is right when one wants it very much. Perhaps I can best explain what I mean and about this book ye are wanting by telling ye a wee story.

"You see," he began, "long, too long ago, two elfin brothers of Eire sat side by side under a giant oak and debated: which is worth more—think ye—the green of the wood or the blue of the deepest sea?

" 'Green gives shade and is cool, quoth I.'
" 'Blue sends fresh breezes and is free, think me.'
" 'Green makes leaves grow wide, quoth I.'

" 'Blue sends up the rivers and seas, think me.'

"And thus me two brothers debated until—so we are told—one turned grass-green and the other sea-blue," concluded Shamus, lowering his head sadly.

"We Broonies know very little more of our origin except that we came into being over a debate. Some say that our cousins the Leprechauns were responsible and that it took place just before the Great Disruption; others claim that it was a century before the Koppelbacks sailed to the Scottish Isles and before the burning terror and captivity. But it is of no consequence to ye, dear Lady. And sorry I am that me memory of these things has faded so."

"But what are we to *do*, Mr. McNutt?" asked Lady Angela anxiously. "It will be certain disgrace for our Society not to be able to produce that book—is there no hope of finding it?"

Looking deeply into the darkness, away from Lady Angela's inquiring face and whistling softly, the little man thought, bracing his chin with his small right hand and putting his left hand on his hip. "Aye, there—is—a—way," he said slowly, "but I'm afraid that it is not allowed to speak of it to ye, only the eldest of our number can tell that story. Still they recite parts of it in song and carve out sayings about our 'missions of helps' on our houses—but ye need not concern yerself, dear Lady, with such things. What is needed is our presence, not a book! Of that I am certain." And he stood firmly, both hands resting on his hips.

"What do you mean, Mr. McNutt, by 'your presence'? We both know that you can come into a household only if the proper 'moments of belief' are evident. But what can a mere child do to gain those?"

"We will see, Me Lady," replied Shamus, bowing three times and extending his right hand. "Come, let us shake in belief, for soon I will depart. I will accept—for ye and yer Society—the challenge. I have reason to believe that much can be done."

Aroused by Lady Angela's sudden return, Mr. Sean-Ticky and the others looked at her crossly for making them wait so long and were about to complain of how cold they were and that it was nearly dawn. But one sharp glance from Her Ladyship silenced them.

Back at the house once again they enjoyed a hearty breakfast which restored their spirits. Then soon they were on their way back to Londonderry, inventing excuses for their wives and housekeepers and even for their cats who would be curious about their absence.

CHAPTER 5

In Pursuit
of the
White Squirrel

"I can't find her; I've looked everywhere," screeched Addie. "Please come and help me, Nemma. Where are you Mary Anne?" Piercing through the hubbub came Adeline Bradbourne's shrill small voice.

"She's forever losing things—that impatient child," sighed the family governess, Miss Nemma Smidgin. "Being in charge of *this* family's domestic affairs can sometimes be impossible."

It was July 1, the most important day of the year for the Bradbournes. Since Easter they had talked, schemed and planned excitedly. Each in his own way dreamed of what would happen to them on their summer holiday at Newport, Rhode Island. Dora, the eldest, who was fourteen, saw herself dancing in glittering lights, the belle of the Independence Day Ball. Carey and Matthew, the twelve-year-old twins, would return to old haunts and new discoveries among the rocks at the seaside. And Addie, poor Addie, thought Nemma, would be getting into everyone's way.

Sighing again heavily, Nemma had no sooner replied to Addie's plea for help in finding her favorite dolly, when Dora poked her head over the banister and complained: "Oh, Nemma, there's a button missing from one of my new white pumps. I simply can't dance without them!"

Reaching the first floor landing, Nemma was just in time to see the rejected shoe flying down the stairs. But before she could get it, Ruffles, the family's West Highland Terrier, had it wedged tightly in his mouth. Off he went, parading proudly toward the kitchen.

"Stop him, Grady. He's got Dora's shoe!" shouted the governess loudly to the cook.

Hurriedly Nemma finished tying the lace sash on Dora's blue brocade dress and placed it carefully in a large trunk.

"Have you seen the twins, Nemma?" called Mrs. Bradbourne from upstairs. "They haven't started to dress. Nemma, where *are* you?"

"They're probably in the conservatory, ma'am. They were washed and dressed an hour ago," replied the governess. "Land knows *what* they look like now," she added under her breath.

Carey and Matthew had been making their own preparations for the family's departure. There were always more interesting things to discover in the garden—giant snails, a discarded robin's egg, bright bugs of all kinds. At the moment they were looking down at a large hole, near the trunk of a giant elm. Some strange creature, which had run through the rose garden and over the small border hedge, had disappeared down the hole. And now both boys defiantly laid claim to the vanished animal.

"It's mine! I saw it *first*," protested Carey, who claimed "first-rights," supposing himself the eldest.

"You did not! I did, and stop pushing or I'll call Dora. Besides, I got here first," whined Matthew, who relied on his sister in matters of dispute.

Suddenly a third rival appeared. Zipping through the boys' legs, Ruffles—still carrying Dora's shoe—plunged head-first into the hole, leaving only his white tail in sight. Frantically, the twins grabbed and pulled, but it was no use.

"I thought you boys *promised* to watch the fish in the conservatory," came Nemma's unexpected voice. Looking behind them squint-eyed, the twins saw the freshly starched colossus of the governess standing over them.

"How could you!" cried Nemma, glaring at their mud-spattered white short trousers.

"But please, Nemma," persisted the boys, "we simply must see it, and Ruffles's gone down. . . ."

"See what?" asked Nemma in a bored tone of voice.

"The white squirrel or whatever it was that came chasing across the lawn," they replied.

But before the twins could finish, behind Nemma came Dora, hopping on one foot, followed by Cornelius and Melissa Bradbourne.

"What seems to be the trouble here, Nemma?" asked the rector calmly.

"Ruffles has gone down the hole, Father," cried Carey.

"And we must get him out," concluded Matthew.

"I'm sorry, boys, but we must start now for Newport," said their father.

"But we can't leave Ruffles here, Father," pleaded the twins together.

"Oh, Mother, can't you do something?" begged Addie.

"We'll be late!" insisted Dora.

Sympathetically Mrs. Bradbourne turned to her husband: "Can't something be done, Cornelius? We really can't leave Ruffles like this."

Cornelius Bradbourne was an understanding man with a practical side as well. In every family crisis he tried whenever possible to take a common sense approach. This would be no exception. The family *did* have to catch the train to Newport and it left the Perry-Dutton station promptly at two o'clock. Yet, Ruffles, the family pet, could not be left in such a predicament. Mr. Bradbourne fingered his stiff clerical collar and prepared for one of his paternal statements. As rector of All Hallows Church he felt strongly his duty. He would have to make a decisive pronouncement.

"Now children," he began, "we can all see that there is only one thing to be done—only one course of action is feasible; if we don't do something at once, we'll miss the train. On the other hand, I know how much Ruffles means to us—I can recall when, as a mere pup, he first. . . ."

By this time the children's attention—as well as Mrs. Bradbourne's and Nemma's—had lapsed. They all stared down at the hole. It seemed as if the domestic sermon would never end.

"Thirdly," continued Mr. Bradbourne, "there must always be a way out of every hole—where there is an 'in,' there must always also be an 'out.'"

Inside the hole, while the rector's dry discourse went on, some strange things were happening. Ruffles had managed to reach the tail of the white squirrel. He buried his nose in its soft fluffy coat, as deeper and deeper the chase continued.

All at once, Ruffles felt himself being pulled downward. With a jerk, the dog slipped from view. Over and over the terrier and squirrel rolled like furry puffballs of cotton through the dark dirt corridor, which was neatly padded with rose and elm leaves. With a thud, they came at last into the tangled under-roots of the giant elm.

From a small opening above, a glint of light filtered down into the hollowed cavern. Chewing fiercely at the web of roots, Ruffles tried to free himself, as the white squirrel delicately wiggled up and out. Turning toward the enrooted and struggling dog, it began to gnaw industriously at the roots. Soon both dog and squirrel were free and the chase cont•ued. Further and further they ran through the underbrush, away from the garden and off toward Crawley Woods.

"Papa, Papa, stop—look!" cried the children in alarm. "Ruffles has disappeared down the hole! We can't see him anymore."

"Why so he has," replied Mr. Bradbourne slowly, disregarding his final point, "I'm sure, however, he will know how to find his way out." And he bent down deliberately to examine the enlarged hole.

The lights of the house had gone out and still there was no sign of Ruffles. "Where *could* he have gone!" cried Carey.

"Perhaps he has found a secret passage or perhaps he found. . . ." speculated Matthew.

"I'm sure it doesn't matter," affirmed Dora, "he's only a dog and good for stealing things anyway—it's *his* fault we missed the train and can't leave for two more days!"

"That's not true, Dora! He's better than any girl, even *with shoes*," replied the twins together saucily.

"I wonder," started Addie, "if he could really have been chasing a Broonie. Grady says that they sometimes visit the garden and ride on the backs of white squirrels."

"Of all the stupid notions," retorted Dora, "Addie, you *are* a fool to believe in such things. Anybody knows that Broonies are like fairies and don't really exist."

For once the twins sided with Addie. "It was something very large and white and furry," they insisted.

"Perhaps Broonies can take different shapes," said Addie quietly to herself.

Silently the summer moon slid through the rolling night clouds. The giant elm stretched and nodded sleepily, its leaves casting dark patterns on the summer house. And before very long the children slept.

36

When the moon was high, Ruffles crawled through the picket fence of the garden, his coat spattered with mud and a limp in his right hind leg. Slyly, he moved toward the elm and began to dig, pushing the dirt back into the hole. Then victoriously he trotted off to the summer house where he often slept when returning from one of his nights out or when he knew himself to be in disgrace. Beside him lay Dora's shoe.

CHAPTER 6

Books,
Books and
More Books

The parsonage on Piety Corner was finally quiet. Grady and Nemma Smidgin sat in the kitchen finishing afternoon tea. Both were exhausted from the family's leave-taking. Grady looked forward to three weeks of uninterrupted freedom from household chores.

"Just think, Nemma!" insisted the cook. "There will be simply nothing to do. I'll sleep till nine, read in the arbor in the morning and go visiting most of the afternoon, except of course I shall be back in time to make tea."

"You certainly will *not,*" rebuked Nemma, "we *both* have work to do. I, for one, must see to The Reverend's books. Have you seen the stacks and stacks in the upstairs hall? I understand that he's inherited his father's collection, and it's quite a size, for Bishop St. John-Lowther was a most learned gentleman. His shelves are already so crowded, how we're going to squeeze all these in, I'm sure I don't know. The manse is looking more and more like the Boston Public Library every day," she added with an impatient sigh.

"Or like old Mr. Sean-Ticky's shop in Londonderry," added Grady, pointing her right index finger at the governess in preparation for one of her "wee stories." "Did I ever tell you the time Mr. Sean-Ticky and Harry O'Neill, the postman . . ."

"No, you did not," protested Nemma, "and now's *not* the time to begin—we have work to do. Off to your dishes now, and I'm off to the study."

Grady started clearing the table. "I never get to tell my favorite wee yarn," she sighed.

"Books, books, and more books," complained Nemma as she reached the upstairs landing, "the place *is* indeed becoming a bookshop."

Leaning her shoulder solidly against the study door, she pushed and pushed, but it wouldn't open. Peeping through the keyhole, the governess gasped in amazement: "The place is literally engulfed in books!"

Again she tried the door, but it wouldn't budge.

"Grady, oh, Grady!" she called. "Come and help me. I can't seem to get the study door open."

Grady left her dishes, hoping for a second chance to tell her story. "What seems to be the trouble, Nemma?" asked the cook, catching her breath.

"The place is so completely booked in that you can't even open the door," exclaimed the governess.

"Here, let me help you," offered the cook.

Together they sighed and heaved, but it was no use.

"There's only one thing to do," ventured Grady, "one of us will have to crawl out on the roof and try to get in through the dormer window."

"But I can't," began Nemma, "it wouldn't be decent and besides, well, I'm far too, well too . . ."

"You *do* look like a Donegal dumpling," teased the cook. "I suppose *I* must do it."

Neatly removing her freshly-ironed apron, Grady sandwiched herself through the narrow hallway window.

"Take care now, Grady! Watch for the slippery moss by the north side of the elm branches," warned Nemma.

Edging herself along the metal outside railing, Grady paused to take a quick look down. Below her, the pastel-colored tea roses sparkled like bright gems in the afternoon light, their delicate heads tossing to and fro. And there, circling in and out of All Hallows Church tower were the neighborhood pigeons ("those nasty birds"), gliding like kites in the breeze.

Cautiously the cook moved toward the protruding side of the dormer window, approaching its slippery side. I simply *must* have one more look, she thought. Holding tight with one hand to the window-ledge and bracing herself against the tree branch with the other, she could barely see the Methodist Chapel two blocks away.

"A little higher and I could see Mr. Keir-Kerry's prize-winning cucumber garden—but what is *that?*" cried the cook in alarm. "Something white flying through the elm branches . . ."

"What did you say?" called Nemma, poking her head out of the hallway window.

"Why you dear creature," said Grady as the white squirrel came scampering up the elm branch, "I do believe you want to help me."

"Grady! Who *are* you talking to?" called Nemma anxiously.

"Oh, Nemma, look!" replied the cook, pointing at the creature.

With a single leap the white squirrel landed lightly on the dormer window-sill, then hopped off again and was soon lost in the foliage of the tree. Grady leaned forward to see where it went, and as she did so, her right foot slipped, leaving her dangling in space. Wildly she clung to the inside sill, her feet sliding up and down on the mossy shingles.

"Help, Nemma! Help me!" cried Grady. "I'm going to fall . . ."

"I'm coming! I'm coming! Hold on!" shouted Nemma.

Forgetting her plea of obesity and that she was fearful of heights, Nemma pulled herself through the window. Teetering on the ledge outside, she picked her way toward the study window. Safely she reached it. Pushing and pulling and steadying one another, the cook and governess crawled, exhausted, into Mr. Bradbourne's study.

"We've made it, we made it, Nemma! Oh, I—I just knew we'd fall," gasped Grady.

"I told you to be careful—who *were* you talking to?" asked Nemma.

"Oh, didn't you see it. Why it's the plumpest squirrel and the whitest I've ever seen."

"Now Grady dear, you certainly don't expect me to believe that you were talking to a squirrel, do you? I think we *both* need a cup of tea."

"But it *was* a white squirrel," protested Grady, "or at least it looked like one. Maybe it was a flying rabbit or some kind of giant. . . ."

"Grady, please stop such nonsense. But look what's happened to the books! They're all unpacked and neatly stacked in rows."

The packing cases and cartons had disappeared—everything was perfectly arranged.

"And the study door is open," added the cook.

CHAPTER 7

Escape
to the
Summer House

Several days before the family was due back in Perry-Dutton, Addie woke up with a terrible toothache. Nemma was immediately sent for to accompany her charge to the family dentist, a Dr. Bull, whom the children called "Rumble-Tummy" because of the noises his stomach made when he bent over them to examine their teeth. The offending tooth was swiftly, but painfully extracted. It was decided that Addie should remain at home until the rest of the family returned from vacation the following weekend.

Miss Smidgin insisted that Addie stay in bed, but after one day she had had quite enough of that.

"I'm fine, I'm really quite better," she insisted, with an eager smile, trying not to wince as another jab of pain went through her mouth.

"I don't want to hear any more arguments, young lady," said Nemma, in her strictest tone of voice. "Dr. Bull gave orders that you are *not* to get up until he has been to see you again," and with that she began to rearrange the pillows behind Addie's head.

"But there's no one to keep me company," said Addie sulkily, "and I'm not ill, not really sick like I was with the mumps." She settled down in the bed while Miss Smidgin gave her a stern and unsympathetic glance that silenced any further protest.

It was a lovely day—too lovely in fact. Addie felt cheated at not being with the twins and Dora. She loved swimming and riding and she kept thinking of how much fun *they* were having, and of how much fun she had had until her tooth spoiled it all. It was unfair that she was confined to her hot stuffy room while they were having such a good time. She felt bad tempered and rebellious.

As soon as she was sure that Nemma had gone downstairs, Addie flung off the heavy robe that she had been forced

46

to wear, yanked off the scarf that Nemma had wound around her jaw and jumped out of bed. Quickly she put on a play dress, a pinafore, and some sturdy shoes. She resolved to play truant and to escape to the bottom of the garden.

"The summer house is so secluded that Nemma will never see me," thought Addie, "unless she comes inside, which isn't likely."

She bunched up some of the pillows under the blankets and closed the heavy shutters on the windows, so that the room was in half-light. If the governess should open the door, she would imagine that Addie had fallen asleep.

Carefully she opened the bedroom door and tiptoed down the corridor to the head of the stairs. In contrast to the children's rooms, which were furnished in white wicker with gingham curtains and cheerful red carpets, the hall was rather gloomy, like the upper floor of the house where Grady and William lived—William being the gardener and Grady's "good man," as she liked to say.

The house had been decorated to be plain and dark at the top floor, becoming lighter and more colorful as one descended. The entrance hall, the parlor, and the dining room were rich and elegant, forming a suite of rooms, each furnished entirely in family heirlooms, which the Bradbournes had brought from Ireland many generations ago. The Bradbourne pieces blended in well with what Mrs. Bradbourne's father had given to his daughter at the time of her marriage.

Despite the formality and good taste expressed, there was something warmly welcoming about the house, with a touch of oddity as well. When old Henry Bradbourne had been rector of Perry-Dutton, before becoming a bishop and before his son had succeeded him, he had insisted that "his rooms," the music room, the study and the library be furnished in his style, which meant a lavish use of Kelly green, his favorite color. Upon his death, despite their disapproval of his taste, his son and daughter-in-law had not dared to alter things, for had they done so the children, who adored "Grandbish," would have issued a loud protest.

As she came down to the second-floor landing, Addie felt more at ease, for apart from her own room this was the part of the house she liked the best. She was beginning to forget the danger she was in, when she almost collided with Miss Smidgin, who suddenly swept out of her mother's dressing room. Quickly, Addie slipped behind the heavy draperies of the landing window. It was fortunate for the truant that her governess was carrying a pile of towels so high that she could not look over them and missed seeing Addie's obvious shape behind the curtains.

When Nemma had disappeared and it was safe to emerge from her hiding place, Addie made her way along the landing and was about to go down the second flight of stairs when she noticed that the music room door was ajar. Usually this room, like the library and study, was always locked. She entered. Everything was still as it had been when her grandfather used to visit the house and they had celebrated Christmas or birthdays together.

Grandfather had been her only really special friend up to now. She sat in his high leather smoking chair, gazed around the room and wiggled her feet up and down absent-mindedly. Then, as she stretched herself and flung out her arms, her right hand knocked something on the small table beside the chair and sent it toppling to the floor. It made a soft thud as it hit the carpet. She slipped out of the chair and knelt to pick it up.

What she found was a small package. It was very tiny, barely three inches in length, parceled in green watered

48

silk and tied with russet velvet ribbon. A bronze leaf was attached to where the ribbon was knotted and there in the middle of this unusual label was her name.

Looking up, she saw the large white squirrel sitting on a limb of the tree outside the open window. She ran across the room to speak to it, but it fled down the trunk and sped across the front lawn. Its shyness disappointed her. She stood for a moment looking after it, and then as she was about to open the tiny package she remembered the danger she was in. Closing the music room door carefully behind her, the gift stored safely in her pinafore pocket, and being careful not to step on the carpet rods with her heels and give herself away, she tiptoed down the stairs, reaching the ground floor safely.

She was just about to open the front door and escape into the garden, when she realized how hungry and thirsty she was. She decided to play one of her favorite games of seeing whether she could get into the pantry for a drink of cold lemonade, a raspberry turnover and some cookies without the ever-watchful eye of Grady spotting her. This escapade was not too difficult, for Grady always sang lustily when at work. As she moved toward the back of the house, Addie could hear her in the kitchen bottling fruit. Several minutes later the young truant reappeared from the pantry with a small basket full of goodies and a glass bottle filled with lemonade. Soon she was outside and clear of the house.

Moving under the shade of the giant elm, Addie reached the safety of the summer house with an excited sense of relief. The mood of adventure—the slight feeling of wickedness at disobeying Nemma and escaping from the sick room—the satisfaction of once again having outwitted Grady, who always imagined when food was missing that she had mislaid or miscounted it—and the discovery of the tiny parcel—all made her feel very pleased with herself. Once inside the little white house, with the blinds carefully drawn, Addie curled up on a cushion on the floor and munching a stolen cookie and sipping lemonade began to open the mysterious package.

She removed the unusual silk wrapping, revealing a tiny book. Wondering who would have thought to use a leaf instead of a paper tag, she examined the strange little volume. It was bound in the same watered silk in which it had been packaged. There was no title on the cover or on the first page, in fact there were no words at all. There were only pictures, a series of small delicate engravings. At once she knew that it was a book about Broonies, for though she had never seen them, the Little People in the illustrations matched exactly what her imagination had conceived them to be like. For a long while she gazed at the eight or ten tiny prints, while slowly a deep longing grew and grew in her.

Finally, shutting the book and holding it between her hands, she closed her eyes and said out loud, "I wish, I wish, I wish that I could see a Broonie *now!*"

Opening her eyes, expecting to see someone, she waited. But there was no one in sight. In disappointment she put the book aside and was sipping some more lemonade and munching the turnover, when a voice said, "Looks very appetizin' to me!"

Forgetting that William, the gardener, was away, Addie thought that Grady's husband was speaking in a falsetto and playing a trick on her. Expecting to see him laughing at the other side of the pane, she ran to the nearest window. But there was no one there.

"William!" she called softly, thinking he was hiding out of sight. "You won't tell on me, will you?"

"But me name ain't William," said the high-pitched voice. "It's Shamus—Shamus McNutt, and what might yours be?"

Addie realized by this time that the voice was not coming from outside as she had thought, but from behind her, from within the summer house. At the back of the little round building was a large cupboard in which the children kept some of their older toys and equipment for garden games. Opening the large doors she saw inside a little man perched on the roof of a large, rickety doll's house, which had once been Dora's pride and joy. His feet dangled over the sides.

"Pity it isn't bigger," he said thoughtfully, as he clambered down. "I could live comfortably in it, if it were just a foot or so larger here and there," he said chuckling to himself. He was only two feet tall, but the toy residence would need considerable expansion for him to get into its rooms, thought Addie. She offered him a place beside her on the cushion, which he readily accepted.

The little man seemed very pleased that the child did not stare at him as so many did when they first saw him. He hated to be considered a "curiosity." True, he *was* small by human standards, and his features *did* seem comical to those not used to Broonies. So it was very pleasant to meet someone, especially a child, who didn't giggle about his nose and ask rude questions about his complexion and his bright red hair. He found himself liking Addie and felt she was warming to him.

He wanted to ask her *why* she had made her wish and tell her the reason for his being there. Addie, too, was inquisitive, but there was a shyness on both sides; so they just smiled at each other, understanding that it would take some time to get acquainted.

"Shall we play a game?" suggested Addie, "How about

dominoes?" And so began a delightful hour in which Shamus tactfully allowed his new friend to win and during which time they consumed a great quantity of lemonade and stolen food. Addie even forgot the danger of discovery, so intrigued she became with him.

But finally her inquisitiveness *did* get the better of her, and in the politest possible tone, she asked, "Mr. McNutt, I hope you won't be offended by my asking, but . . . well . . . where do you come from? And how do you happen to be here? And well . . . what kind of person *are* you?" As if to apologize for being so forward, she held out a piece of chocolate toward him which she had been saving for herself. Readily he accepted.

"Capital stuff this!" he said, munching rather noisily. "Haven't had anything so good since the reign of Queen Anne."

"When was that?" asked Addie.

"Two hundred years ago," he said matter-of-factly and then, seeing the look of concern on her face, began to explain to his young companion how this could be.

He had come into being, he told her, in the tiny hamlet of Groonie Glen in Brackenshire, near the Western Isles of Scotland. He had spent his boyhood there until his seventeenth year, when the great "Calamity" came upon his people. First of all, there was the terrible plague which had swept over the entire country, and which weakened his people so much that when their enemies came they were helpless to protect themselves.

"What kind of an illness was it?" asked Addie sympathetically, feeling a sudden twinge of pain in her jaw where the tooth had been pulled.

"The most fatal of all," said Shamus gravely, "Pyrrhonism—no one believed in us, and a Broonie has to be believed

52

in to keep his strength. Otherwise he turns green, loses his remembrance of things, and falls asleep for long periods of time. I myself was born somewhere between 1670 and 1700 as far as I can determine, but since that time I've had only about forty waking years.

"But to answer yer question about Pyrrhonism, 'twas a terrible thing, it was. It all happened because some ninny wrote a book denouncing us as superstition. So, great numbers of people, who had previously relied upon us for the things that only a Broonie can do, lost their confidence and renounced their faith in us."

"Oh, how terrible," Addie interjected.

Shamus continued, "Then on a fateful day that I can recall but dimly, the Koppelbacks of Grimmelgower attacked the clan while most of the menfolk were off on a hunting expedition. We were all of us still weak from the great sickness, so that had we been there we could have done little to resist them. When we returned home and found our loved ones gone, we trudged after them, tracing their tracks in the snow. But we soon became lost and could not find our way back to Umbrie. And so in fear of the giants and wishing to go where the plague could not infect us again and where we might find those whose faith could restore our strength, we sailed across the sea and came to Ireland where our cousins, the Leprechauns, looked kindly on us and gave us a home in the Seton Woods of Londonderry."

"But why did you come to me and not my father?" asked Addie, "I'm only ten years old, you know."

"Ah! but the younger ye are, the easier it is to believe, my child," said the little man with a warm smile. "And besides, yer father is away, and if he's a typical grown-up, he may resist such a notion as believin' in the likes of me. Furthermore, when I was dozin' here in the summer house, me sleep was interrupted by a young lassie, whom I distinctly heard wishin' to see a Broonie *now!*"

Again he smiled, and it was the warmest, most kind look she had ever seen. His face flushed a bright orange and his eyes flashed with eager excitement. Then his features became more serious as he thought of his task.

"Addie, me love, I can't say how happy I am that ye longed to see me. But there are many that do not care about such things. I've taken a great risk, ye know, coming here, me child, for everyone who could give me strength could also take it away. We Broonies grow more powerful for everyone who accepts us, but for every rejection, we 'diminish'—as we say—and start to fade. Sometimes I fear that our task is too big for a single Broonie!"

"Oh, but I'm willing to help!" Addie blurted out, "and I'm sure that many of my friends and my father and my mother and brothers and sister and Nemma and Grady and William and Grandma will all want to know you the moment I tell them how we've met."

"I wouldn't be too sure of that," said McNutt. "Not everyone has a heart as young as your'n," and he patted her head with his tiny hand.

The two of them were suddenly startled by a noise from outside. Nemma was marching angrily toward the summer house with Ruffles barking close at her heels. Addie crouched down hoping for a miracle. She was surprised to hear McNutt utter a strange sound like a tea kettle beginning to boil. A moment passed, and a skunk appeared from under the summer house, followed by several of its offspring.

Ruffles stopped and then backed off, warily sniffing the air. He seemed afraid to bark. Nemma, seeing the skunk ahead of her, shrieked and, running toward the kitchen,

54

shouted to Grady, "The garden is infested with those nasty striped creatures."

Quickly Addie urged McNutt out of their hiding place and, realizing that he was only a fraction of her size, took him piggy-back through the trees, in through the front door and up to the nursery, not forgetting to keep a careful look-out for the governess and the cook.

"By St. Patrick and St. Andrew!" exclaimed a breathless McNutt, once they had reached the safety of Addie's room. "That *was* a close one!"

And Addie agreed.

CHAPTER 8

The Twins Grow Curious

Addie sat quietly in the nursery. If only Mr. McNutt had left some sort of calling card. That was what troubled her most—how to convince the rest of the family that her dear friend lived with her in the nursery. They had had such a brief acquaintance, but already she missed him whenever he was off on one of his nightly "help missions," as he called them.

Meanwhile in the kitchen Nemma and Grady were having another of their arguments over the children.

"No! they *cannot* have cookies and lemonade *before* dinner," said the governess decidedly for the third time, pointing her finger at Grady. "The Rector and the missus are having guests for dinner tonight and I won't have you spoiling everything."

"But Nemma," insisted Grady, "they haven't had a treat since returning from holiday. Surely *one* cookie and a small glass of 'ade wouldn't hurt anyone."

"All right," sighed Nemma as Grady quickly reached for the cookie jar, "they may have *one* cookie each and a *small* glass, no more—and my name is 'Miss Smidgin' before the guests, *Mrs. O'Grady!*"

Grady walked briskly (her head thrown back) toward the large conservatory where the twins sat playing marbles. The cook could never understand *why* Nemma took herself so seriously. One would think that the entire fate of the Bradbourne household (and, in fact, all of Perry-Dutton) rested on her starched shoulders.

Carey and Matthew hardly noticed the cook as she approached. They had just come to the crucial point in their game of black-and-whites.

"How about a treat for the winner?" asked Grady. "I have been given special permission to offer," she hesitated, with a wink, "*one* cookie and a glass of 'ade each."

But neither of the boys responded.

"There, that makes me ten to your nine," said Carey.

"But I still have one more shot," interjected Matthew, moving closer toward his last black marble.

A long silence followed as Matthew took aim. The most important rule of black-and-whites was that during a player's turn there was to be absolute silence. Carey and Grady watched intently. Suddenly the black marble shot out, hit the white one on its right side and darted off into a far corner of the conservatory and struck a metal stand supporting a large Australian fern.

"Now look you here, boys," rebuked Grady. "I've told you to mind Grandmother St. John-Lowther's favorite fern and your father's aquarium. Isn't anyone willin' to take me offer?" she asked again, lowering her voice. "I might even make it *two* cookies each," she added.

"I will!" shouted Matthew.

"Me too!" joined Carey, "I'm the winner, you know."

"Let's include first runner-up as well," suggested Grady, turning to leave.

Slowly through the conservatory doors came Addie, her eyes downcast.

"Now what's troublin' you, dearie?" asked the cook.

Addie stood, looking down at the boys. It was hard to put into words how she felt about Mr. McNutt.

"What's wrong, Addie?" asked Carey.

"Have you lost something again?" taunted Matthew.

Both boys looked quizzically at her. "I want to tell you something," she began, "but you must *promise* not to laugh. Please say you won't."

"All right, Addie, we promise," said the twins together.

"Well, the other afternoon I had a strange visitor. Actually he has become my very best friend, and I want you to know about him. His name is Shamus McNutt, and he looks something like the wee folk. . . ."

"The wee folk," laughed the twins, "and I suppose he told you about a pot of gold or promised you barley sugars or a new doll," said the twins together.

"But you *promised* not to laugh—please, oh, please don't, how can I make you believe!" Addie said, turning away in despair.

"I know!" exclaimed Carey, "why not take us to *see* your wee Mr. McNutt. That should be easy enough."

"Yes!" agreed Matthew, "where does he live—in a tree?" he asked with a chuckle.

Quickly they decided that Addie should show Shamus to the twins. They left the conservatory and soon were on their way down the long upstairs hallway, leading to the nursery. Outside the door, Addie paused. "Let me go in first," she pleaded, "we don't want to frighten him."

The child slipped slowly inside. Everything was as she had left it. Her favorite doll, Mary Anne, was sleeping in her crib, the small table was set for tea, and the dormer window open. But her friend was nowhere to be seen.

Peering anxiously through the window, she called softly. "I need you, dear Mr. McNutt. *Please* come and show yourself to the twins."

Gently the evening breeze fluttered through the thin white curtains. Addie parted them again—but there was no sign of the Broonie. The same slight wind stirred the giant elm branches outside the window as Addie waited. In the distance came a faint whining drone of pipes. And with a series of windy spurts the strange tune filled the nursery. Turning toward the doll crib, Addie saw her friend perched on the side, his legs swinging in rhythm to the music.

60

"Oh, Shamus, you did come!" she exclaimed. "I knew you would!"

"Hello there, darlin', you were lookin' in the wrong place. I've been here all the time," replied the Broonie, tossing his head. Addie ran toward him with her small hands extended.

Suddenly there was a noise at the nursery door. Bursting into the room came Carey and Matthew, shouting, "Where is he? Addie, we want to *see* the king of the wee folk." Running to the window, the boys were just in time to see something white bound from the sill to the elm tree outside and scurry up into its branches.

"Is *that* McNutt?" asked Carey. "It looked like a white squirrel to me!"

"Or like the creature in the garden," suggested Matthew.

"It was . . . he is . . . I mean you simply must believe that he was here talking with me. . . ." As she pleaded, Addie's eyes filled with tears and running from the crib, Mary Anne in her arms, she hugged the China doll and buried her face in the folds of its white linen dress.

"We believe, we believe, Addie, please don't cry. Come back!" called the twins after her. But Addie ran down the hall to the stairs, through the conservatory and out into the garden.

Looking down at the hole by the elm tree, she whispered, "Are you there, dear Shamus? Please come back, I won't let the boys hurt you."

But there was no sign of the Broonie. The wind continued to flutter the roses, scattering their petals through the garden and among the marigolds. Addie could still, very faintly, hear the lilting tune as it faded.

"Mary Anne," said Addie turning toward the summer house, "we *will* find him and we will make them believe!"

CHAPTER 9

Someone to Blame

By the time December came McNutt had become Addie's constant companion. He slept in Addie's doll's house beside the toy cupboard and ate a strange assortment of foods which his young friend smuggled up to him from the kitchen. He longed for an oatcake and marmalade and for a decent cup of hot tea. But, as the one was unheard of in the Bradbourne household and tea something the children didn't drink, he had to be content without either.

Three days before Christmas, a time when Addie was usually tense with excitement, she felt disinterested in the holidays and had to admit to herself that she was very discouraged. She had tried so very hard to persuade the other members of the family to accept McNutt's presence, but they thought of him only as a figment of her imagination—"another of those childish games," said Dora, "that she will eventually outgrow."

Already five months had passed and if something didn't happen soon, McNutt would begin to fade and would be gone by the time fall came. The little man was obviously as worried about it as she was. But they refused to speak of the subject for fear of upsetting each other.

The family was enjoying Sunday dinner in the dining room. It was the best time of the week for everyone. Mr. Bradbourne was always in a good mood, with Morning Worship over and an afternoon nap ahead of him before Evensong. The roast beef Grady had prepared had been especially delicious, and her molasses pudding with custard sauce a culinary delight which all had enjoyed. Everyone felt fully satisfied. As Mrs. Bradbourne was pouring coffee, her husband began disclosing plans for the Christmas celebration.

"I have long thought," he began, gripping his lapels as if another sermon was coming on and repeating the phrase for added emphasis, "I have long thought that it would be doubly exciting if instead of *one* Christmas tree this year, we should have *two*. We'll have the usual affair in the drawing room. But why not have another one in the hall?"

Everyone agreed that it was a splendid idea, until Mrs. Bradbourne pointed out that the front hall was crowded, while the children's grandmother suggested that in "a proper Bostonian household a single tree is quite sufficient."

But Mr. Bradbourne was quite determined. He pointed out that the staircase was constructed in a spiral which provided a spacious stairwell. "A tree," he insisted, "could easily be placed there, provided that it is tall and slender."

"But the branches will poke through the railings of the banister," complained Matthew.

"And tickle our ankles as we come down the stairs," giggled Carey.

"That's part of the plan," said their father. "You see, the idea is this: we'll put our bigger gifts—those that we open on Christmas Day—around the base of the tree. And then on the branches, we'll place a small gift for each member of the family, for each of the twelve days of Christmas, so that as the holidays pass the presents will become higher and higher up the tree, until those for the very last day—the final surprises—will be at the very top.

"As we go to bed each night, we'll sing *The Twelve Days of Christmas* and then we'll lean over the banister and take our package for that day. Now here's a box with all our names in it. Each of us must pick a slip and then prepare the presents for the person listed."

Looking around the table, Mr. Bradbourne could see that his inventiveness met with the approval of everyone. Even

Grandmother St. John-Lowther nodded, though somewhat reluctantly.

On the last day of school the rector and William went off in the sleigh while the children were still at Miss Mullett's Academy. When the youngsters arrived home there was the usual tree in a tub in the parlor. Another more impressive evergreen stood in the hall. It was tall, slim and erect. Beginning in front of one's eyes, it rose almost out of sight to the second story landing. Its branches were so full that—as the twins had predicted—the larger branches brushed against the banisters and protruded through the posts.

As soon as supper was over, William marched with ordered precision into the hall, carrying a stack of light wooden boxes in which ornaments were kept. Grady, Nemma and the children's mother—as well as the youngsters themselves—had been busy for days making gingerbread men, colored fairies, Santa Clauses and other little figures from almond paste and sugar. There was a profusion of candle holders and tinsel and icicles and ornaments, delicate bubbles of glass and tiny tapers for lighting the tree. With everyone working feverishly, the task of trimming the tree was finished by nine o'clock.

As they sat around sipping mulled cider and nibbling gingerbread men, everyone agreed that this year they had outdone themselves. Addie, Carey and Matthew were beside themselves with excitement, their faces aglow with delight, wondering what the various boxes might contain.

Suddenly Mr. Bradbourne exploded, "Why, bless my soul!" he shouted, "we've forgotten the star for the top of the tree."

After searching for several minutes, the missing ornament was finally found. Climbing the stairs, the children's father reached the second floor landing. Leaning over the rail, he could see the tip of the evergreen, but it was too far for him to reach it easily. Whistling rather blithely, he clambered over the banister and with one foot lodged between two of the posts and gripping the polished balustrade with his left hand, he reached toward the topmost point of the huge tree. His hand was about to drop the star on the vertical stem, when the maid's zealous polishing had its effect. His left foot skidded on the smooth stair, his body lurched outward, and losing his balance the rector of All Hallows Church decorated the Christmas tree with his own person.

Down he came, his arms flailing, his hands grabbing at the branches. To everyone's terror he made a most undignified descent into the hall, landing with a resounding thump on top of the pile of presents around the base of the trunk. It was immediately determined by an anxious Mrs. Bradbourne and an equally concerned Nemma that no bones were broken, although the rector was severely shaken. Rubbing a few bruised places on his body, he looked around at the tragic faces of his family. Then, realizing his ridiculous posture, he broke into uproarious laughter. Soon everyone joined in the merriment and assisted him to his feet.

"I think somebody pushed Papa," said Matthew impishly.

"And I think it was McNutt!" responded his brother, casting a wicked glance at Addie.

With a mischievious glint in his eye, Mr. Bradbourne began inventing a jingle—it went:

> "It must have been old what's 'is name,
> I'm sure that he's the one to blame,
> It must have been old what's 'is name,
> It must have been McNutt!"

The twins thought a minute or two and then began improvising:

> "It must have been old you-know-who
> Who got us in this awful stew.
> If it wasn't me, and it wasn't you,
> It must have been McNutt."

Gradually as they said the words and everyone joined in
the fun, a tune began to emerge, so they sang the verses
through again in order to remember them. Then Mr. Bradbourne and the children's mother made up some more lines.

> "One minute I was on the stair.
> The next—the stair, it wasn't there,
> And I was flying through the air.
> Down I came with quite a rush!
> Who was it gave me such a push?"

Everyone howled with laughter at this and then waited
for someone to finish the song. Suggestions were made
and rejected, until Grady and Nemma and William came
up with:

> "It must have been old thing-um-a-jig,
> Or someone who is none too big,
> It must have been old thing-um-a-jig,
> It must have been McNutt!"

William was very proud of himself for having suggested
the word "thing-um-a-jig," and Nemma was flushed with
pride that she knew how to spell it, when the rector began
scribbling down the words. He read them out. Everyone

laughed again. Soon they were singing it all through with Dora playing the melody on the piano in the drawing room, and everyone else dancing and laughing and crying all at the same time.

All except Addie. She stole quickly away to the nursery, trying hard to put on a happy face for her friend. Arriving at the landing to her floor, she saw him sitting up against the base of the grandfather clock.

"So you heard," she said sadly. "I was hoping you wouldn't. Oh, Shamus, dear Shamus, what does it take for them to believe in you?"

"A miracle, darlin'," he said, patting her head with his tiny hand, "a good old-fashioned Irish-type miracle, that's what it takes. And we'll see one yet, you can be sure of that, or me name's not Shamus McNutt!"

It must have been McNutt

1. It must have been old what's 'is name,
2. It must have been old you – know – who,
𝄋 It must have been old thing-um-a-jig,

I'm sure that he's the one to blame,
Who got us in this aw - ful stew.
Or some – one who is none too big,

It must have been old what's 'is name,
If it was – n't me and it was – n't you,
It must have been old thing-um-a-jig,

It must have been Mc – Nutt.

Words and music: Bryan Jeffery Leech.
©Copyright 1974. Used by permission.

One min-ute I was on the stair,

The next — the stair, it was-n't there,

And I was fly-ing through the air.

Down I came with quite a rush!

Who was it gave me such a push?

CHAPTER 10

A Most Unhappy Easter

Rapidly the months passed. And although April came in with a chill as if reluctant to leave March behind, the sun shone brightly. A brisk wind bent the first snowdrops to the ground. It was Easter morning.

Sunday at the Bradbourne house was not a day of rest. It came and went in a rush and bustle. Mr. Bradbourne was up at six and conducted early communion before he came to breakfast. His appetite was ravenous—he always consumed two extra eggs and at least three cups of coffee when facing the demands of leading worship. Like everything else in the rectory, meals were always punctual. But on the first day of the week, the rule was relaxed and Grady served the family one by one as they straggled into the dining room. The younger children were tripping down the stairs when they heard a commotion coming from below. Their father was loudly complaining to the cook—something he rarely did—that his second egg was "almost raw!"

Such a calamity had never happened before, and Grady was so busy defending herself that she forgot about the rolls in the oven. Suddenly the smell of smoke from the direction of the kitchen sent her rushing madly toward the stove. With a fierce sigh, she lifted out the charred pieces.

"It must have been old what's 'is name," she muttered to herself bitterly.

As Matthew and Carey entered the dining room, they found Mr. Bradbourne nervously tapping his saucer with a spoon, and he too was blaming Addie's friend for the disastrous breakfast. The twins were helping themselves to porridge, molasses and milk when Dora came running in from the hall.

"William was harnessing Grizelda, the mare," she announced, "when she broke free and jumped the wall. Now she's heading down High Street! William's chasing her!"

Immediately Mr. Bradbourne sprang to his feet and, grasping a large walking stick from beside the front door, he ran out of the rectory, calling for William who by this time was already losing ground behind the horse. Spring having finally caught up with her, Grizelda had no intention now of returning home.

Gradually William slackened his pace and, waiting for his master to catch up, abandoned the chase for the moment. Breathlessly they plotted how to ensnare the wayward animal. They could barely see her disappearing into Crawley Woods, the rector's favorite riding spot. Once inside the trees, she would be impossible to find.

Enlisting the assistance of several small boys, William and the rector continued after her. On reaching the wood they saw no sign of her. While they debated what to do next, the church bell began to ring in the distance. Alarmed, Mr. Bradbourne glanced at his pocket watch, suddenly realizing that it was almost time for morning service.

Dashing back toward the town, he sped past members of the congregation who—with the service about to begin—were astonished to see their rector sprinting down the High Street. Nodding rather oddly to them as he passed, Mr. Bradbourne hurried to the parsonage. Taking care to adjust his clothes and wiping his forehead before entering, he tried to gather his thoughts before worship. His wife attempted to calm him as he pushed past her on the way to his study.

"Oh, dear, where are they?" groaned the rector, donning his vestments. "Where *did* I put my notes?" And then remembering having put them down during the early communion and that his spectacles were beside them on the lectern, he entered the sanctuary.

It was apparent to his wife and children that this was

not to be the usually well-ordered service, which had become the Reverend Bradbourne's trademark. His voice was shrill and shaky as he gave the opening prayer, and halfway through the Lord's Prayer his mind went totally blank. Everyone noticed that he was no longer leading worship. Members of the congregation glanced at one another during the hymn, sensing their rector's bewilderment. During the announcements, he tied the events of the next week into a hopeless knot. Then several small boys in front began to titter when, putting his hand absentmindedly into his pocket, he drew out a table napkin placed there during his sudden exit from the dining room.

Mrs. Bradbourne closed her eyes during the sermon and prayed for the conclusion. Her husband was usually so bright and interesting, especially at Easter, but this morning his address was full of embarrassing pauses and nervous glances at the notes before him, as if he were unable to make sense of them. Mercifully the service ended. But as the congregation stood with bowed heads for the benediction, they were startled to hear the rector say, "For what we are about to receive, may the Lord make us truly thankful."

Suddenly realizing that he had said the table grace instead of the closing blessing, Mr. Bradbourne stammered and stuttered, overcome with shame. Staring blankly at his people who had now opened their eyes in amazement, he blurted out disjointedly, with a look of devastation:

"It must have been old what's his name;
I'm sure that he's the one to blame;
It must have been old what's his name;
It must have been McNutt!"

The congregation stood paralyzed. What on earth had

possessed their beloved clergyman! Dr. Parrot, the family physician, looked apprehensively at the rector and expected him to collapse at any moment. Stunned, Horace Wheeley, the organist, forgot to play the postlude, and the choir tittered with suppressed laughter.

As the people filed out of the church into the morning sun, instead of admiring new hats and dresses and wishing everyone a "Happy Easter," the topic of conversation was the rector's health. What *had* he meant by "It must have been *McNutt*"? Certainly no one could recall a member of All Hallows Church by that name. On this they all agreed.

At the parsonage, lunch was served but everyone ate in silence. Even Mrs. Bradbourne was afraid to question her husband. When dessert was on the table, Mr. Bradbourne finally looked up, smiling weakly, and asked if William had found the mare. Grady reported that she had been finally found asleep beside an oak tree, exhausted from the chase. William had ridden her back to the stable.

"I've never in all my life known a day so full of calamities," said the rector. "It's simply incredible!" he exclaimed. "What *will* the parish think of me?"

But then recovering his sense of humor, he began to laugh about his mishaps. "Perhaps there really *is* a McNutt," he suggested jokingly.

"Perhaps there is," said Addie, wishing fervently.

"Oh, no! there isn't. It's just a silly game," put in Matthew.

"It's a silly, silly game," chimed in Dora and the twins as they chanted the jingle teasingly.

Addie bit her lip. She wanted to protest, but managed to remain silent. She realized that arguing would convince no one. McNutt himself had told her that debates never end in friends. Instead, she asked to leave the table and ran upstairs to see him, his lunch concealed in her napkin.

CHAPTER 11

A Small Conspiracy

Addie sat down beside Shamus. He was tucked away in the window seat and looking down into the garden where Ruffles was chasing one of the skunks and getting the worst of it. He turned toward her and when he saw the bundle in her hand, smiled eagerly, licking his lips in anticipation. She spread out the contents in front of him with an air of pride, to which he responded with a gasp of delight, pronouncing it "a hearty feast fit for a laird!"

Shamus ate heartily and with considerable noise—the one thing which Addie didn't like about him. But she discovered that talking to the little man made her less aware of his noticeable crunching.

"Something's got to be done," she said desperately as McNutt began devouring a large chicken leg. His face took on a bleak expression as he put the tasty drumstick down.

"Aye," he agreed, "we're in a pickle, 'tis true indeed, if something doesn't turn up soon. I confess to ye, darlin', that this one has me stumped good and proper. Ye know, in a sort of way, they *do* believe in me. I mean they're always chatterin' about me, aren't they?

"But so far, I'm only a convenience for them; an excuse for the foolish and thoughtless things they do. It's not exactly the kind of welcome I'm lookin' for, to be treated as a scapegrace and to be insulted mornin', noon and night."

Shamus paused, returning deliberately to the chicken leg. For several minutes they sat in silence while McNutt finished his lunch with mouthfuls of Grady's caramel pudding. All of a sudden McNutt put down his spoon, slapped his tiny thigh and exclaimed, "I've got it, an idea, Addie, me love! Whenever me old grandmother was in a puzzle about this or that she'd always utter a rhyme that never failed to help. It went something like this—

" 'When one mind's done its thinkin'
And nothin's comin' through,
Then a single brain is not enough,
So you'd better try two.
And if two do nay better
And the riddle is nay solved,
'Tis clearly indicated
That a third should be involved.
Which simply proves the proverb
As constant as the sun,
That two or three or four heads,
Or five, six, seven or more heads
Are better, much better
Much better than one.' "

"Now Addie," said Shamus, "is there someone of yer knowing, someone who's—as me blessed father used to say—'Fearful with the Above and cheerful with men'? Someone who could advise us in a case of this sort?"

"Why, of course!" exclaimed the child excitedly, "why didn't I think of him before! Mr. Keir-Kerry is just the man. I think he's Scots and Irish. It was he, in fact, who first told me about the Little People. He used to be the caretaker in father's church. He's retired now and lives in a cottage near Crawley Woods. I think he's just the one!"

Angus Keir-Kerry was not surprised to have a visitor that afternoon. Nor was he shocked to discover that Addie had left the house without permission. Angus was nearly seventy-five, but in spite of his wrinkled face and swan-colored hair, his eyes danced with youthful gaiety. His voice, which seemed always to be singing, was vibrant and clear. He did not need to recall what it was like to be six or ten or fifty, for he was able to assume any age he chose. And thus he had won the friendship of almost everyone in the village,—except of course Mrs. Sinclair Cabott, III, who didn't like children and thus didn't like him.

There were times when his zest and high spirits got him into trouble and when, in some people's opinion, his prank-ishness went too far. As caretaker he had often joined in baseball games which took place on the common across the street from the church. One day, four summers before, he had been at bat and had hit the ball with such force that it sped through the air and hit the west side of the chapel. It landed with a crash in the middle of a large stained-glass window depicting the martyrdom of St. Adolphus the Good who, in Queen Mary's reign, was beheaded in Coventry. The ball struck the saint squarely on the nose and the impact shattered the colored panes, sending a shower of glass on top of the baptismal font.

St. Adolphus didn't seem to mind, for when his features were put back together, he still had the same rapturous expression as before. But the parish council viewed the incident less kindly, and it was suggested at the next quarterly meeting that a new verger be hired—one who "would attend to his work and refrain from boyish pranks."

As he was several years over sixty-five, Mr. Keir-Kerry was glad to leave and amuse himself with his cottage and vegetable garden which brought visitors from as far away as Harvey Green and even Boston. So famous was the size of his squash and hothouse cucumbers.

Addie's friend would never think of starting an important conversation without brewing a pot of strong Irish tea and cutting large slices of his favorite Dundee cake. Addie liked both, especially the tea which she didn't often get at home, and because Mr. Keir-Kerry didn't ration the amount of sugar lumps the way Nemma did.

"I wonder if he will believe in McNutt," thought Addie, as she posed the case of a friend of hers at school who found herself being blamed for things at home. She asked him how *he* would deal with such a problem.

Angus ate his piece of cake and sipped another cup of tea before he spoke. "I'll grant," he said thoughtfully, "that it's hard not to be appreciated, but there's nothin' new in that. I m'self could complain that no one ever thanked me durin' me years of cleaning and tidying up the kirk. The moment I beheaded a glass saint, I got the sack.

"That's hardly appreciation, now is it?" he paused, looking deeply at Addie. "But child, ye have to forgive and forget." And he took another sip of tea.

"You know, Addie m'dear, that's the way so many treat the good One above. Why He does so many fine things for them, but the only time they seem to mention Him is when something goes wrong.

"Calamities they call 'acts of God,' if you please. Well, now, isn't the risin' of the sun and the singin' of a bird and a smile on a wee one's face an act of God, too, I ask ye? Of course it is . . . but no one seems to recognize that!"

Putting his hand on Addie's small shoulder, he concluded, "So your friend isn't the only one who's being put down. But I *do* have an idea for ye that might work. How would it be if your wee friend—did ye say it was a girl at school?—*if* your friend were to think up all sorts of helpful things to do? Maybe then her family would begin wonderin' just who it was that was being so kind. By the way, that young lady wouldn't be you, would it Addie?"

"Oh, no, Mr. Keir-Kerry, it's a friend of mine. It's not a girl though, not someone at school. It's someone at home."

"At home," Mr. Keir-Kerry said, obviously surprised. "One of the servants, Dora, the twins?"

Addie shook her head, and then took a deep breath. "His name is McNutt . . . and . . . and . . . he's a Broonie."

"A Broonie, is he?" Mr. Keir-Kerry stirred his tea thoughtfully.

Addie went on. "Do you remember the story you told me about the Little People and about the cobbler of Marne who didn't know how to mend shoes and who asked the Broonies to mend them for him? And how he was found out because the little men sewed on soles and heels that did queer things to the people who wore the shoes? Some shoes, you said, made them dance; others made them run.

"Well, I never forgot that tale. And I heard Grady say, 'It's a bad day for the Broonies.' Then I found a book full of pictures of the Broonies in their homes and at work.

"So I wished I might see a Broonie for myself, and suddenly there he was—Shamus McNutt from Seton Woods."

Addie drew the tiny silk-covered book from her apron pocket and handed it to her friend. He took it very carefully. His eyes examined each of the pictures very slowly and very carefully, and then he looked up at Addie.

"I've always been interested in tales of the wee folk," he told her, "ever since me granny told me about them. And I've always had a suspicion, just a suspicion mind you that the legends *might* be true. I've a friend who insists that she's seen plenty of them, but she's so eccentric I've never known whether to believe her stories or not."

He glanced at the tiny book again. "You say that you had the wee volume in your hand, and you just wished to see a Broonie and there he was. Is that how it happened?

"Well, I'm going to do the same thing, Addie, I've lived a full number of years and there's too many things in this life that can't be explained for a man not to believe in those whose work is unseen."

84

Addie repeated exactly what she had said in making her wish. Mr. Keir-Kerry then took the book in his hands and closed his palms together with the little volume between them. In a hushed and solemn voice he wished that he, too, might see a Broonie *now*. He and Addie opened their eyes and there was McNutt standing on top of the small wicker table, his right hand extended toward Mr. Keir-Kerry.

"Pleased I am to meet ye, sir," said Shamus with a courtly bow.

"Likewise, I'm sure," said the delighted gentleman in reply. "And welcome to me humble abode," he added, offering to make McNutt more comfortable by improvising a chair for him from some books and a soft down pillow.

When McNutt was settled, Angus poured some tea for him into an eye bath—it was the only thing he could find of the right size—and offered him some cake. McNutt was in a very cheerful mood, and Addie saw that the greenness she had been noticing lately had completely disappeared from his face. His cheeks were glowing red-orange and his features seemed more animated than usual.

"I've been sittin' here since Addie arrived," said McNutt, "hopin' that yer heart was young. And it is, for anyone who believes in Broonies has to be a little like a child. It's a simple trust that is required, y'know. 'Tis happy I am to hear yer advice as to what I should do in attemptin' to persuade Addie's family."

The three of them began to plan some of the things that a Broonie might do to help the Bradbournes. It was Sunday afternoon when Addie was supposed to be taking a nap in the nursery and an ideal time for a visit to Mr. Keir-Kerry. But there was no time to lose, they decided. McNutt must begin his new campaign tomorrow morning.

CHAPTER 12

The Strangest Things Do Happen

It was Monday morning—Mr. Bradbourne's "day of rest." The grown-ups ate an hour later than usual, but the children, now on holiday, were already off riding their penny-farthing bicycles up and down the lane behind the rectory. Mr. Bradbourne announced to his wife over coffee that he intended to spend the morning in his study cataloging his father's collection of rare books and exploring the latest batch he had ordered from Mr. Sean-Ticky. He had not had time yet to look over the books Nemma had unpacked for him.

As soon as the grandfather clock struck ten, he marched into his favorite room in the house, his study, and shut the door solidly behind him. Soon he was immersed in the volumes neatly arranged by topics on the shelves.

"I must remember to thank Nemma for doing such thorough work," he murmured to himself.

The rector of All Hallows Church had one fatal flaw—an incurable absentmindedness. Thus he spent the morning relocating his spectacles, picking up and misplacing his pencils and pens, and sometimes even losing his handkerchief. By the time lunch was served, he had a fully developed case of irritation with himself.

But when he returned to his desk that afternoon, strange things happened. When his glasses became lost, his hand seemed to find them immediately. His pencil actually rolled across the desk toward him. He didn't want to mention it to his wife, but he could have sworn that his handkerchief came flying through the air like a bird, landing gracefully in his chest pocket. And his quill pen popped itself back into the inkwell, the moment he turned his back. All of this put him in such a good mood that when he came to supper, he fairly glowed with satisfaction. Proudly he boasted of how *he* was overcoming his forgetfulness.

He was mentioning this when, rather disconcertedly, he saw a large burnished leaf drop silently into his soup. "Where on earth did *that* come from?" he asked, looking up at the ceiling. Addie concealed a knowing look by sipping some more broth from her bowl.

"Incredible!" said her father, dipping his spoon again.

"It is rather strange, Cornelius, that you should mention your improvement in finding things," remarked his wife. "I, too, have been most encouraged today with a problem that has always troubled me. You know the difficulty I've always had remembering people's names—well, today Nemma and I were in the Waterkin Emporium buying muslin for Dora's new dress, when in walked a Mrs. Devereaux and her three unmarried cousins, who are here for a short visit from Braintree. I was introduced to them only a week ago and, for a moment, couldn't recall a single name. Then Blanche Curtis came in and I had to introduce them— my mind went blank. Suddenly, when I concentrated hard, the names returned. Perhaps, dear, it's just the effects of spring rejuvenating us!"

Mr. Bradbourne agreed.

His wife was helping Grady serve the dessert course—a custard pudding the children had demanded—when a gust of wind blew open the window, sending a shower of bronze leaves over the table. Her husband sprang to his feet, announcing with finality, "So that's where it came from!" He picked up one of the leaves from the carpet and studied it for a moment.

During the week that followed all sorts of incredible things happened in the rector's house. Grady accidentally left a saucepan on the stove. It was full of hollandaise sauce and, try as she would, she could not get it clean. Setting it down in despair, she started another of her chores. Coming back to it an hour later, she found the pan bright and gleaming in the sink. "Fancy me forgetting that I'd scoured it," she muttered to herself. Another golden leaf fell in front of her, but she ignored it, thinking it had dropped out of one of Nemma's floral arrangements.

The next day Mrs. Bradbourne consulted with Nemma and Grady about the arrival of guests for the weekend. She handed Grady a list of those who were expected, indicating the room each guest was to occupy. Inwardly Grady groaned. Company meant more work—airing mattresses, ironing sheets, cleaning upstairs windows, beating carpets—there was no end to it!

That afternoon she and Nemma, who in addition to minding the children gave a helping hand when guests were expected, went up to the second floor. As they opened the first bedroom door, there came a gentle rush of air. The windows had been opened. The glass panes sparkled from fresh cleaning. Bedwarmers were inside each freshly made bed. And a vase of roses stood on a side table near the writing desk. The two women looked at each other, but neither said a word, each fearful that the other would accuse her of having a hallucination.

Mrs. Bradbourne joined them and, seeing the condition of the room, thanked them for working so hard and so quickly. They accepted her appreciation without comment. They were giving the furniture a final inspection when they both noticed, among the narcissus and tulips in the bowl in the hallway, a single brownish leaf cleverly woven into the arrangement. Nemma plucked it out of the cluster of flowers.

"These things seem to be everywhere," she complained.

Grady felt uncomfortable but said nothing.

Walking into the garden on his way to the vestry in the

church, Mr. Bradbourne happened to glance back at the parsonage. He had only yesterday mentioned to his wife (and to the church council the evening before) that the exterior of the house needed paint. He himself was rather partial to changing the color to a muted Puritan green, a shade that was all the rage in Boston. And there it was— done! The woodwork glistened with soft, fresh paint. He had revealed his intention to William and had told him to order the materials, but he was amazed to see the task already finished. After the disaster of Sunday morning, it was good to see that there could be days when life went along swimmingly.

"And yet, it *is* odd," he said thoughtfully, looking down at the bronze leaves on the path in front of him. "Here it is spring and not one of the trees is shedding!"

Later that day the rector thanked William for his prompt action and, although he looked rather stunned, William nodded, pleased to receive the commendation.

Matthew and Carey had decided to spend their holiday building a tree house at the very back of the large yard, close to the kitchen garden. Dora, in a condescending mood, had offered to help them. They were clad in their oldest clothes and were equipped with saws, hammers, ropes and numerous gadgets.

Feverishly they worked all day, trying to make a suitable foundation for the structure. They securely fastened planks and pieces of an old crate to the forked center of the main trunk of the large elm. Their work was hampered, however, by the sudden arrival of showers that afternoon.

Looking out from the nursery window, Dora and the boys were dejected by the gusts of rain and the delay caused in their project.

During the night the bad weather erupted into a storm

that shook the house. The wind howled in the chimney, and lightning flashed through the windows. With the first clap of thunder, the children were awakened. Peering out into the garden, they could just make out the elm tree—but the boards were gone! The tree house lay in a heap on the ground. With sighs of dismay, they returned to their warm beds.

"I told Dora her plan wasn't good enough," said Matthew irritably.

"I knew it wouldn't work," agreed Carey. "That's what comes of having a girl involved. Girls don't know how to do anything *practical."* And with that final pronouncement, the twins fell asleep.

Matthew was the last asleep, but the first to wake. The sky had cleared. The sun took up its place in the sky. Walking uncertainly toward the window, still half asleep, Matthew looked out to inspect the disaster. But to his surprise, instead of a heap of rubble at the foot of the elm, he saw nestled in the branches the most magnificent tree house he had ever seen. It rose like a rustic minaret through the uppermost branches. There were observation platforms, little portal windows, rope-operated entry ways, and on the very top a flag with a green thistle emblem on it. Soon he and Carey were busily pretending they were chivalrous knights at Camelot.

When the family assembled for breakfast, the boys insisted on everyone inspecting their new achievement. Their father pronounced it "grand," and their mother even dared to climb up to the first level.

"What ingenious sons we have, Cornelius," she remarked.

"They get it from your brother Edwin, my dear, that's obvious," her husband returned. "You know how clever *he* is at making things."

Leaves by the handful came cascading down on top of the Bradbournes, but they brushed them aside indifferently. Matthew and Carey basked in parental approval. But neither let on that he had had nothing to do with erecting the tree house. Addie remained silent.

CHAPTER 13

The Plot Thickens

The dogwood budded early. After days of expectation Addie finally caught the pinkish-white buds popping into bloom. Saturday would be May 30. Running from the garden toward the conservatory, with a sprig locked tightly in her small hand, she called excitedly, "Nemma, Grady, it's time for the picnic!"

Breathlessly she burst into the kitchen, leaving the doors swinging wildly behind her. Nemma and Grady, however, were too involved in a heated argument over the proper care of African violets to pay any attention to the child's intrusion.

"Now look you here, Nemma Smidgin," retorted Grady. "I've cared for the family violets for over ten years now, and I won't have you tellin' me how much to water them."

"I only said, Grady dear, that you water them far too much—one would think you were carrying on a baptismal rite!" replied the governess.

Ignoring Nemma's last remark, Grady turned to Addie. "Child, what in the world is it?" she asked.

"Oh, Grady—look Nemma! it's time for the May Day picnic. Please ask father to name the day, Nemma! He *always* listens to you!" she pleaded.

Smiling with half-concealed pride at her self-importance, Nemma spoke authoritatively, "I'm glad someone listens to me in this household. I will do what I can." And with a quick glance at Grady, who now faced the row of violets on the kitchen window sill, she added, "It *would* be nice to go on a picnic, wild flowers can't be spoiled like potted ones." And she hurried out of the kitchen with Addie close behind.

Afternoon tea progressed as usual. The general parish talk (adult talk to the children) continued dryly: should the old gardener be re-hired—would there be sufficient funds for the new organ—would Bishop Plunkett approve this or that.

Addie found herself lost in thought. When *would* Nemma mention the picnic? Talk, talk, and more talk. Finally it came. A third cup of tea had been poured and Mr. Bradbourne paused, reaching for the last slice of gingerbread. As Nemma picked up the empty cake plate, she began, "Sir, I have noticed just this morning that the dogwood is starting to bloom—will the picnic be on Saturday?"

There was a slight pause. The children held their breath as Mr. Bradbourne contemplated. Then he replied, "I can see no reason why it should not be this Saturday—yes, we will all go to Milton Pond on *Saturday*. Make all the arrangements, Nemma. And Melissa," he added, turning to his wife, "be sure to invite Grandmother St. John-Lowther. It wouldn't be the May Day picnic without her." All were agreed. With Addie, the twins and Dora chattering at once, tea ended.

That night Addie left the dinner table early. She had somehow to get in touch with Shamus and tell him about the picnic. Of course he couldn't miss it. She sat a long time in the nursery, waiting for him to come, but—alas—he didn't.

"Oh, now Shamus," cried the child, "I know you're here somewhere, you can't hide from *me!*"

But the Broonie did not appear. Finally it was time for bed and Addie went sadly to her room. Suppose her friend failed to hear about one of the greatest days in the entire year, she thought to herself.

Sleep carried her off into dreams. She saw Milton Pond with its groves of pines and thickly planted water reeds. It was so very dark that she could hardly see the small lake. Suddenly the moon passed from behind a cloud. Addie turned restlessly in her bed.

"Why, *why* had Shamus not told me he had to be away!" All at once she felt something soft and furry near her cheek. Slowly she opened her eyes. There above her, hanging on the headboard of the bed with its long bushy tail dangling over on to her face, was the white squirrel.

"Oh, you have come! Shamus must be near, will you tell him about the picnic for me?" she asked.

The squirrel looked intently at her, so deeply in fact that Addie felt herself being drawn into its pool-black eyes. Floating into them she went deeper and deeper. Silently it slid down on to the pillow beside her and began, with some effort, to raise her head.

Before she knew it, she was at the window; slowly she pulled aside the thin white curtains. Then she climbed on the sill and seized the tail of the white squirrel. With a sudden leap, the animal jumped out of the window, Addie floating after him. With all her might she clung to its long bushy tail, as together they flew through the moonlit night. Below her, Addie could see the parsonage and All Hallows Church—she could even see, in the distance, Mr. Keir-Kerry's vegetable garden.

Suddenly, almost as quickly as she had left the window, Addie found herself falling ever so fast and, with a light thud, she landed on the bough of a large white pine. Next to her, his legs crossed and whistling a strange tune, sat Shamus.

"Me darlin', ye are right on time, so glad ye could come," he said jokingly. "I didn't want ye to miss the grand gathering!"

"I'm so frightened, Shamus, whatever will I do if I fall?" queried Addie anxiously.

"Now never ye mind, me darlin'," he reassured her, "just

ye hold tight to the tail of me friend—he can always be trusted."

And then, waving his tiny hands and standing up on the branch of the pine, the Broonie began making wild gestures, as if to a large company. "To the left, Mr. Raccoon. Step more to the right, Mrs. Mallard. Ye may sit in front, Mr. and Mrs. Bin-Robin. Make way for Cheese-Bit."

Looking below her Addie saw all the animals of Milton Pond—raccoons, squirrels, large ducks, other smaller birds, mice (one of these must be Cheese-Bit, she thought), badgers, two deer and a fawn, not to mention many smaller animals, who hid behind the trees. Expectantly they waited for Mr. McNutt to address them.

Standing nimbly on the branch, he began, "I have called you all here, me friends of Milton Pond, because, first of all, I should like to thank each of ye for yer services. Ye have all done yer jobs splendidly. But I have yet one grave favor to ask ye."

At the word "favor" the ducks began to quack loudly, "What, what, what," and a young fawn pranced over to hush them up, sending the flock into a flutter.

"Silence, you feather-heads!" spoke up a dignified coon who immediately took the role of judge.

Shamus raised his hands in protest. "Listen! dear friends, I beg ye to hear me out. As ye know, I am a stranger in yer woods, but ye have received me kindly, and I will relay yer kindnesses to our brothers and other kin in Seton Woods, when I return.

"We Broonies, as ye know, are a sad folk now, since we were forced into exile by the Koppelbacks of Grimmel-gower. They compelled us to leave our blessed homeland of Umbrie, so that we fled for sanctuary to our cousins, the Leprechauns, across the great sea to Ireland. We suffer still, at times, because of our skin—how often we have tried to regain the brown color of our ancestors." At this point Shamus lowered his head sadly, extending his small hands which, in the moonlight, had a greenish hue.

Mr. and Mrs. Bin-Robin chirped softly to each other, "We understand, we do, we do—how hard it is to fly away every year, only to return in the spring."

Nodding his head in appreciation, McNutt continued, "But we, the Broonies of Seton Woods, have a high calling. We have gone on many happy missions and have had great victories (I cannot tell all—they slip from mind). I myself have been sent, as ye know, to the Bradbourne's in Perry-Dutton. I came because I was wished for by the youngest member of the family, wee Addie here, and accepted the challenge put to me by Lady Angela Foggerty.

"Now dear folk, Addie needs all of us. For ye see her family still doesn't really believe, and if they don't do so soon, I will be too weak to return home. How forgetful are humans—always recalling their troubles but rarely thinkin' of their jolly times," asserted the Broonie, with downcast eyes.

"How sad, indeed, how very sad," chattered the animals in unison.

An especially portly looking owl shifted her weight and opened one eye knowingly.

"*Who* does not believe, I say? Who, who?" she hooted.

Shamus raised his hands again and spoke, "Only dear Addie, me darlin', and our old friend Mr. Keir-Kerry believe in me. But I have devised a plan which will prove, once and for all, to the Bradbournes that I Shamus McNutt, visited their town and lived in their home. Will ye help me?" he asked and sat down quietly.

There was a very long pause as the animals waited,

considering the Broonie's request. Then the owl opened her eyes widely and hooted bravely, "Who will say, 'No'? Who, I say, who?"

"We are all agreed," replied the coon solemnly. "We will help if we can, but what must we do?"

The meeting ended with Shamus thanking each comer individually. After things had quieted down and he was alone except for Addie and the white squirrel, he began whistling in a soft high-pitched tone and put his arm around the neck of the little animal.

"Me friend," said Shamus, stroking its snowy fur, "how lonely I would be without ye—so many jolly times we've had together—if only ye could speak, like the others, and tell us of our past.

"Methinks ye recall that stormy night in the glens of Grimmelgower when our people fled to the Crystal Cave. How they sat warming themselves by the fire that wild night."

The white squirrel looked up longingly into Shamus's deep blue eyes. It seemed to reassure him.

"Come, friends," said McNutt finally, "it is time we should be getting back." Holding onto the fluffy tail of the giant squirrel, Addie clung tightly to it and to the hand of McNutt behind her. Flying high above the pine-tops, the sturdy animal towed them safely over the woods. And before Addie could look down, they were at the nursery window.

Letting go of the squirrel's tail, and with Shamus on her shoulders, she dropped into the room. It was dark. But before very long she had nestled her friend snugly in the doll's house. And with high excitement she returned to her bed, forgetting that she had not invited the little man to attend the picnic.

But Saturday was cold and wet and the picnic had to be canceled. Mr. Bradbourne was just as disappointed as everyone else, so as a compensation he had William drive the family to the station and took everyone to a theater matinee in Boston. In all the excitement of this sudden change of plan, Addie forgot about Shamus. But later, when she did think of him in the middle of the performance, she suspected that someone from the Seton Woods would not have enjoyed "Little Dorrit" quite as much as she did.

CHAPTER 14

A Beastly Recital

Since his first day in Perry-Dutton, Mr. Bradbourne had dreamed of providing the church with a new organ. The sanctuary itself was lovely, its plain New England whiteness offset by rich stained-glass windows. Everyone who entered to worship was inspired just by being there—that is, until Horace Wheeley began to play. Not that he was at fault, it was just that the instrument was so old and so inadequate that it wheezed, spluttered and coughed out its notes like an old gentleman with a chest cold. All remedies had proved inadequate. It would groan and shudder at the most inappropriate times, especially during lengthy prayers, convincing the rector and organist alike that it had a secret life of its own.

It had not taken long for Mr. Bradbourne to determine what had to be done about it. With considerable impatience, he had waited for the money to be raised and for a new instrument to be built and installed. Finally, however, when it was finished, he set to work planning a special day for the dedication of the new instrument, complete with bells and a harp. Mr. Bradbourne's dream was to have a recital by Dr. Beardsley Bush, the well-known concert organist from the Beacon Hill Conservatory. There were some members of the parish who thought their rector was aiming too high, but when the distinguished virtuoso consented to come and when the bishop himself agreed to be present, they were full of admiration for the idea.

Everyone of note in Perry-Dutton was invited. Distinguished guests came from Boston. New clothes were ordered specially for the occasion. House parties assembled in all the larger homes to make a celebration of the entire weekend, starting with the concert on Friday afternoon and concluding with the annual picnic on Saturday. The Boston newspapers even sent reporters to cover all that was happening. Perry-Dutton held its breath, for never before had this gentle, little town felt itself to be so important.

When the great day came Cornelius Bradbourne was in a froth of excitement. He couldn't keep still. He checked and double checked the arrangements, getting in everyone's way. In the chancel he almost overturned the large vase of flowers which the decorations committee had prepared for the altar. His wife tried to calm him, but it was no use. The children had never seen their father so excited, so agitated, so much in a dither, nor had they seen him rush around with such speed before. One minute he was in the church, then in the house, and next back in the garden again to inspect the large tent which had been erected as a refreshment marquee. He was dressed in his new black suit fully two hours before it was necessary.

"Oh, do get along! We shall be late, they'll be here any minute," he called up the stairs at least once every quarter of an hour. But no one took any notice of these unnecessary warnings.

The day was perfect for June. The dogwood was now in full bloom. The air serene and balmy. As the first carriage drew up in front of the main door, Mr. Bradbourne dashed madly through the library, up the stairs in search of his wife, and failed to notice that she and the children had assembled punctually in the front hall and were waiting for him.

"Oh, there you are," he gasped, when he eventually sighted them from the first landing. Running down the stairs by two's, he bounded across the hall and out through the front door to meet the early arrivals.

An hour later the church was packed with people. The seats in the chancel area were reserved for honored guests, among them Bishop Plunkett and his wife; the Mayor of

Boston and his large family; Senator Collingwood, his wife and mother; and the local Perry-Dutton officials, together with all the Bradbournes. Addie sat beside her grandmother in the front row on the left side in full view of the new organ.

And there it stood, ready to make its first official sounds, its pipes in full array. At last as an expectant quiet came over the audience, Dr. Bush came in through a side door, walking deliberately with the calm assured step of a master. Slowly he seated himself on the bench, adjusted some stops and, nodding to the assistant standing beside him to open the book, began to play. Soon everyone was transfixed by the exquisite music filling the church. For the first time that day Mr. Bradbourne relaxed and, squeezing his wife's hand, smiled at her contentedly.

The recital had been in progress for about ten minutes when, during a very quiet passage of soft flutes and the prized harp-bells, a window up on top of the nave burst open with a loud bang! The congregation was momentarily startled, but soon became lost in the music again. They did not notice that the culprit was a large owl who was now entering through the opening. He flew down to a cross-beam and surveyed the scene.

The owl was then joined by several companions who came and perched beside him. Next six blue jays swooped in through the aperture and, being less cautious than the owls, began to circle the entire sanctuary, skimming over the heads of the people, narrowly missing them by a few inches. Several children were silently scolded for looking around. Their parents pretended not to notice the odd intruders.

Plucking up his courage, one of the owls glided down to the lectern close to Mr. Bradbourne's pew. The rector was aghast and tried to shoo it away as best he could. It began to hoot out its high call in a loud and very audible song of defiance, ignoring Mr. Bradbourne.

A rook and its mate flew down and, settling on top of the organ pipes, began to sing a noisy, "Caw! caw! caw!" in time to the melody that Dr. Bush was endeavoring to play. Other smaller birds were now present, fluttering and diving above the heads of the congregation. However, being proper Bostonians and notable citizens of Perry-Dutton, they remained stiff and erect, hoping that by ignoring these unruly creatures, they could persuade them to go away. But the birds were having a fine time and showed no intention of leaving.

The ushers at the main door were so busy trying to decide what could be done about this appalling situation that they failed to notice a large column of animals marching in through the south entrance. There were rabbits, moles, badgers and skunks, mice riding on lizards, and chipmunks, several dogs of the town, a number of cats, and a very large lone raccoon, leading them and other animals—all squeezing in through the narrow opening where the door had been left ajar. Then spilling into the side aisle came a rush of animals and leaves. Helter-skelter they ran, in and out of the pews and under the feet of the startled parishioners.

One of the mice, a plump little fellow carrying a bit of cheese, ran forward into the choir area, clambered up the organist's stool, then up his back and sat comfortably on Dr. Bush's shoulder. Nervously the organist looked at it. With a sudden jerking motion he tried to knock it away, while at the same time playing a difficult passage. The mouse did not move. But Dr. Bush's right hand slipped, striking the keys sharply. He winced at the wrong notes and glared at the tiny animal. And then played on desperately.

Meanwhile another and even fatter mouse had climbed up to the first manual and was noisily skipping up and down on the keys, in competition, it seemed, with a hefty badger who thumped regularly on the foot-pedals—boomp! boomp! boomp!—moving them up and down. Organist and rector exchanged helpless looks with the bishop and all three glanced angrily at the head usher. But the situation was clearly impossible.

The children in the audience were convulsed with laughter, but they dared not show it, knowing how the slightest guffaw would land them in serious trouble. They had come prepared to find the concert dull and boring, but it was turning into the greatest lark they could imagine. And yet it was an agony for them, especially for Addie, for the expression of her father's face distressed her, and she knew inside who was responsible. She kept whispering under her breath, "Oh, Shamus, you really *did* it this time!"

By now the ladies were squirming in their seats to avoid the mice. A few tried valiantly to suppress a scream. It was the skunks who finally brought the concert to an abrupt halt. Hopping up onto a pew, they bounded blithely along the seats, jumping from lap to lap of the astounded and terrified people.

Suddenly, as if the joint reserve of the entire audience was exhausted at once, pandemonium broke loose. Women fainted, ushers swatted at animals, children cried because their parents were blaming them for encouraging their pets to follow them to church. The bishop stood up indignantly, fixed poor Mr. Bradbourne with a disapproving glare and, beckoning to his wife, began to leave.

Mrs. Plunkett prepared to follow him, unaware that one of the blue jays had settled on top of her large, wide-brimmed hat. As she moved to get up, the bird—suddenly disturbed—deposited an egg amid the tulle and ribbons. As she turned to give Mrs. Bradbourne a final curt nod of farewell, the egg rolled forward and over the brim, landing with a smash on the skirt of her dress. With a shriek of rage and kicking at a badger who happened to be standing in the entrance to the pew, she and the bishop made a furious departure.

The other special guests ran hurriedly from the church to their carriages and ignored the pleas of the rector to stay for the celebration tea that had been so carefully arranged. Eagerly the Boston reporters pushed ahead of the audience. It seemed to Mr. Bradbourne that everyone, including the bishop was blaming him for what had happened. Inside the tent the hospitality committee waited in vain. A few loyal parishioners, sensing the bitter disappointment of their rector, looked in and smiled weakly at the Bradbournes. Not knowing what to say, they all left without having even a cup of tea.

CHAPTER 15

Old What's 'is Name Appears

The children were sentenced to an early bedtime that night, but before they were sent upstairs Mr. Bradbourne gathered them together in the library. He had not spoken to them after the concert for fear of losing his temper, but now that he had calmed down, he wanted to know *why* they had planned such a cruel joke. In his mind the entire affair was a large-scale prank which the youngsters of the parish had plotted together. His own children were hurt by this accusation and swore their innocence.

"I don't know how you could suspect *me* of such a thing," said Dora with an indignant look at her father. "I'm not a child, you know! How could you imagine that I would want to spoil your beastly old concert!"

She would have left the room if her mother had not beckoned her to stay. Her anger subsided into tears.

The twins remained quiet for once, not daring to say a word. Although they had had nothing to do with the crime, they had enjoyed it so much they felt guilty and suspected they looked it.

After Mr. Bradbourne had questioned them for several minutes, demanding answers to his doubts, Matthew blurted out, "We didn't do it, Papa, and anyway we couldn't possibly have trained that many animals and birds to act like *that!*"

"And besides, we don't have pet skunks and owls and blue jays," added Carey.

At this point, Mrs. Bradbourne, who seldom disagreed with her husband—at least in front of the children— remarked, "You're jumping to conclusions, Cornelius. The animals and birds involved were mostly *wild* creatures to begin with, and *they* couldn't have been responsible. And who could have opened the window in the nave to let them in?"

114

Addie, too, was questioned. But, as she pointed out, several people would have had to be involved in order to herd so many animals into the church and, as her father well knew, the children and all of their friends had been present inside the building during the recital.

In exasperation, Mr. Bradbourne looked at his family as if begging for their help. "Well, *someone* must have done it. It didn't just *happen*," he said bitterly, recalling his disappointment and embarrassment of that afternoon.

There was a long pause and then Addie spoke, almost in a whisper:

"It must have been old what's 'is name,
I'm sure that he's the one to blame;
It must have been old what's 'is name,
It must have been McNutt."

Mr. Bradbourne was about to tell her to leave the room, that this was no time for silly games when he saw the seriousness of her expression.

"Papa," she said, summoning all of her courage, "you said that *someone* must have done it. And that someone must be a person with a power over animals. You've heard Grady say that a Broonie living in a forest learns how to talk to all the creatures who live there. Isn't that true?"

"Well, yes, that's true," said her father uncertainly, "but if there *are* Little People—and I'm not quite convinced there are—they live in Scotland or Ireland, and they never, to my knowledge, have been found in New England."

"But Papa," said Dora, surprising Addie by coming to her aid, "if they *do* exist, surely they could emigrate just as Grandfather and Grandmother did—or as Grady did. After all, she's Irish but she doesn't live in Ireland."

"And there's Mr. Keir-Kerry," put in Addie, "He lives here, but he'd be very insulted if you called him anything but Scots-Irish."

"That's not the point, my dears," said the rector, still unconvinced. "We know that our ancestors moved here from other parts of the world, but there's no evidence that the Little People have ever strayed from their homeland."

"But supposing that one of them was just looking over a ship in a harbor and accidentally got trapped on board," suggested Carey.

"Or was clapped in irons and kidnapped," added Matthew who had read too many adventure stories. "He could find himself in any part of the world, and why not in New England!"

Picking up the enthusiasm of her brothers, Addie said with all the persuasion she could muster, "But it *is* possible, it is, isn't it, Papa?"

Mr. Bradbourne had to agree that there was no reason on earth why a Broonie or a Leprechaun might not visit the New World. He admitted, however, that there had been few who had claimed to have seen one, and these had all been Irishmen who were, as everyone knew, quite prejudiced about them. Their claims had been dismissed as being nothing more than over-imagination or the effects of too much whiskey.

Addie asked to be excused from the room. She returned a few moments later with the tiny book in her hand. Without a word of explanation as to how she had come upon it, she handed it to her father, who was at once intrigued by the strange, wordless book. His wife and the other children gathered around him as he turned the tiny pages and studied the pictures of the Broonies of Seton Woods.

Finally, they looked up and Addie knew that her chance

had come. Secretly she wished that McNutt would help her, that she would say just the right things. Her father had always been affectionate with her, but Addie knew better than to disagree with him, especially when he was in an angry mood. And yet, here she was daring to speak out at what seemed like the worst possible moment for a discussion.

"Father," she started boldly, "there *is* a Mr. McNutt. He's quite, quite real. And you have seen signs of it. Remember how quite suddenly you stopped being absent-minded, and instead of losing your glasses you were able to find them every time you needed them? And remember how when you were congratulating yourself for this, a strange leaf fell into your soup?"

"Well, yes, I do recall that," said Mr. Bradbourne rather uneasily.

"It was McNutt who kept finding your things for you, and it was he who dropped the leaf. I saw the leaf, but only McNutt could have told me about your glasses and your pens."

"Mama," interrupted Dora, "you saw some of the leaves, too. Remember when you were telling us how you'd suddenly improved in recalling people's names?"

Mrs. Bradbourne looked down at the floor in embarrassment. Grady and Nemma began to confess that someone had been helping them with their household chores and that they had taken the credit for it. They, too, had noticed the mysterious golden leaves.

"We didn't dare to speak of it, even to each other," said Nemma, who was very disturbed to have Addie see that she, too, could err. And then she added, rather weakly, "We thought we were seeing things."

Grady was more honest. "For all of my talkin' about

Broonies, it was just a game. I never suspected for a moment that a real little person was busyin' himself to help the likes of me," she said.

Addie looked across at Matthew and Carey, who were unusually quiet. They avoided her gaze. She waited, then slowly and reluctantly the two boys confessed that they had had nothing to do with the magnificent tree house in the giant elm. They hung their heads as they admitted that they had taken all the praise while doing none of the work. Dora, too, looked sheepish.

"Papa," said Addie after a long silence, "I tell you on my word of honor that I knew all about these things before you and the others confessed them, because Mr. McNutt told me. Doesn't that convince you that he's real?"

Her father was about to say something, but she went on. "Oh, Father, Mother, Dora, Carey and Matthew, and you Grady, and you dear Nemma, wouldn't you like to know my friend McNutt? He's so kind, so much fun, and he needs people like us to believe in him. . . ." And she went on to explain the reason for which her friend had come to New England.

When Addie had finished, she slipped down on her knees, with the book of pictures in her hand and holding it toward them she invited them to kneel with her and to make a very special wish. They gathered around in a circle with bowed heads and closed eyes, each with a finger touching the watered-silk binding.

"I believe in Broonies," they said in chorus, "and I wish to see one *now!!*"

Suddenly the French windows blew open with a bang. The lace curtains billowed out like the sails of a wind-jammer, and the room filled with bronzed leaves which danced about their heads and then, as quickly as they had

118

come, disappeared into the fireplace and up the chimney.

The Bradbournes were still blinking with astonishment at this when they saw McNutt. He was wearing an outfit that Addie had never seen before, an emerald-green velvet coat with silver braid trimmings, a cocked hat with a large red ostrich plume, and at his side a jeweled dress sword. His complexion, she noticed, was the brightest orange-brown she had seen yet, and his eyes fairly bulged with exhilaration.

As no one spoke, he said finally, "Well, Addie, me darlin', ye'd better introduce me to them."

And he went on, smiling warmly at the Bradbournes. " 'Tis a strange thing," he continued, "about ye humans. Yer so good at blamin' anyone but yerselves for the foolish and wicked things ye do. Now what's so bad about ownin' up when ye do somethin' bad or when ye hurt someone? Is it so hard to admit what ye are—very human persons—and to say that yer sorry for it? Makin' up with the Above and makin' up with men can be mighty pleasant, indeed it can!

"And learnin' to be grateful fer the gifts He gives ye every day, now there's a virtue! There's none of us, ye see, who can manage by ourselves, we all need the gifts put inside others. So let's take our own blame in future and remember to give credit where it's due."

As he said these words which sounded like a wee Broonie sermon, a light mist entered the room. One by one heads nodded and soon all the Bradbournes, together with Nemma, William and Grady, were sleeping.

When they awoke an hour later, McNutt was gone and so was the tiny picture book. They searched all through the house, but neither the quaint little fellow nor the precious collection of pictures which had helped to bring him to them could be found.

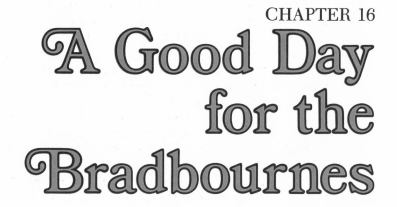

CHAPTER 16

A Good Day
for the
Bradbournes

Finally Mrs. Bradbourne suggested a light supper. The family moved into the dining room where Grady had prepared hot milk and honey muffins. As they were pulling up their chairs to the table, the mysterious white squirrel bounded into the room through the open French doors and, hopping up onto Addie's lap, began to caress her hands. Then he jumped on to Carey's lap and did the same to him, and on from person to person, until he had shown his liking for each of them. When he came to Mr. Bradbourne at the head of the table, he settled down comfortably and went to sleep.

Smiling down at the squirrel, the rector began to give thanks for the meal. He had hardly said, "Our Father," before the strangest commotion broke out all over the house. It seemed to start upstairs with the grandfather clock. Then all the clocks, and there were plenty of them, went wild in an instant. The Friesland Hood wall clock immediately behind the children's father began—one, two, three, four, five, six, seven, it chimed. Everyone looked up for the minute hand had pointed to 9:45 only a short while before.

And then they noticed that all the other clocks were doing the same. The full-calendar, moon-phase grandfather in the hall, the French wag clock in the study, the Eli Terry piece in the drawing room, the small bracket in Mrs. Bradbourne's dressing room, the alarm clocks in the servants' quarters—all whirred and buzzed in reverse and clanged frantically like the percussion section of the Perry-Dutton village band.

Carey ran outside to take a look at the clock in the church tower. He came back full of excitement. "It's going backward, too, Papa, come and see," he reported.

Mr. Bradbourne ran out into the yard and through the gate into the street. He caught the sound of the chimes coming in on the wind from Harvey Green, the next parish, near Milton Pond. And there, too, time was rolling backward.

"Why bless my soul," exclaimed Cornelius Bradbourne excitedly under his breath—and then he blessed his soul for a second time.

The sun began to rise in the west as the hours spun back to afternoon. Was it happening all over the world? Were watches and church clocks all feverishly changing? Was Big Ben adjusting itself in London, just as the pocket watch in his waistcoat was doing? And what of the town clock in Londonderry? Was it, too, moving backward like the clock on the steeple of All Hallows Church? Suddenly it stopped. In Perry-Dutton it was two in the afternoon.

Running back into the house, Mr. Bradbourne yelled out gleefully, "It's light outside, it's light outside. It isn't ten o'clock in the evening; it isn't tomorrow; it's today; it's this afternoon! Look, Melissa, the carriages are beginning to arrive. And there's dear Mrs. Thompson bringing her delicious scones for the celebration tea. Come, hurry, my dears, get your best clothes on again or we shan't be in time to greet our guests."

"It's a miracle, Cornelius!" said his wife.

"A good, old-fashioned Broonie-type miracle," laughed Addie.

As the bells rang out and the birds sang, the Bradbournes welcomed their friends to the recital. They smiled to themselves to see that the bishop and the other important guests of the parish were quite unaware of what had happened.

As they sat in their pews, waiting for Dr. Bush to make his entrance, the white squirrel slipped unnoticed down the aisle until it came to where Addie sat. Soon it was comfortable in her lap. The Bradbournes exchanged jubilant glances and someone whispered, very faintly of course:

> "It must have been old what's 'is name,
> I'm sure that he's the one to blame;
> It must have been old what's 'is name;
> It must have been McNutt."

And then the recital began.